SNAKE OIL

When gambler Jack Morton invests his winnings in the wagon and stock of a snake oil conman, he reinvents himself as Professor Cornelius Murgatroyd, purveyor of a miraculous cure for rheumatism. Travelling across the West making a precarious living from the gullibility of others, his life is disrupted when he promises a dying woman that he will take her baby son to safety with the child's grandfather in Claremont, several days' ride away. Morton must pit his wits against numerous adversaries to fulfil his promise — and stay alive.

FENTON SADLER

SNAKE OIL

Complete and Unabridged

LINFORD
Leicester

First published in Great Britain in 2016 by
Robert Hale
an imprint of The Crowood Press
Wiltshire

First Linford Edition
published 2020
by arrangement with
The Crowood Press
Wiltshire

A catalogue record for this book is available
from the British Library.

ISBN 978–1–4448–4372–9

Published by
F. A. Thorpe (Publishing)
Anstey, Leicestershire

Set by Words & Graphics Ltd.
Anstey, Leicestershire
Printed and bound in Great Britain by
T. J. International Ltd., Padstow, Cornwall

This book is printed on acid-free paper

1

In a tea chest at the back of his van Morton kept a fat diamondback rattler. Rattlesnakes were, as you might say, his stock-in-trade these days, but the one that he carried with him on his travels was next door to being a pet. Of course, he regularly picked up other rattlers for use in his show, but that great diamondback — a shade over four feet long — well, that was special.

Eighteen months ago Jack Morton had been scraping a living by playing poker on the steamboats that plied the Mississippi. Since some of the towns in that part of the country had strict anti-gambling ordinances, the river-boats were where the action was if you wanted to play cards publicly with a bar near at hand, and maybe a pretty girl or two looking over your shoulder. The only problem was that there were many sharks working those waters, in comparison with whom Morton was a veritable minnow. If he made enough to keep himself in liquor and cigars he reckoned to be doing well enough. That was until the night that he had his big win: the win that had set him up in his present business.

The boat was moored in some little tributary of the mighty river, picking up cotton from the plantations thereabouts. A bunch of men had come on board that night, determined to throw their money around. Morton had held his own and then had come that fabulous hand: a nigh-on unbeatable four knaves. Everybody else had dropped out until there was only him and one other left in. When they finally showed it was to discover that the other man had the best species of full house you could hope to see: aces over kings. It was no wonder he'd been betting so high, but it wasn't enough to match those four knaves of Morton's, and he'd cleared a little over $2,000 on that one hand.

He wasn't a one to press his luck when fortune had smiled on him to this extent, so Morton had gathered up the money and prepared to go back to his cabin. The man who'd had that full house followed him and for a moment Morton thought that there was going to be trouble.

'You was mighty lucky there, friend,' the fellow said.

'Well, it happens. It's rare enough as a hand like yours'd be beat, but there it is. That's the luck o' the draw.'

'Oh, I ain't complaining,' said the man hastily, 'I just thought you might be a man as had an eye to a good business opening for your winnings.'

Morton laughed at that. 'Tell you the truth, I'm not a whale at business. I reckon I'll stick to this cash money. I know where I am with that.'

'Well, why not let me buy you a drink and tell you what I'm offering. You don't lose anything by that and who knows, it might be to your advantage.'

Offhand, Morton could see no reason not to go along with the scheme. He was a dab hand at spotting those gamblers who were part of a syndicate, working in concert to fleece unwary players, as well as those types who befriended well-off men in order to rob them when once they were intoxicated. This man wasn't of that brand and it was still fairly early. Besides which, Morton could do with a whiskey to celebrate his win. So he agreed and went with the other to the bar.

Once they had drinks in their hands the man, who introduced himself only as Abernathy without saying if that was his Christian or surname, set out his pitch.

'It's like this, sir. I came here today to raise capital for a venture in which I'm interested; it don't signify what. I badly need that two thousand dollars you won tonight. There, you see, I'm a-laying of my cards down so you can see how I'm fixed.'

Jack Morton stirred uneasily.

4

'Well, I'm sorry and all for your misfortune in losing,' he said, 'but that's how it goes sometimes. I won and you lost. I don't feel guilty about it and I ain't about to part with any o' my winnings for a sob story.' He made as if to leave.

'Not so hasty,' said the man who'd given his name as Abernathy. 'Lordy, folk round here are right suspicious. I'm not asking for your charity. I'm offering to set you up in a profitable, going concern that will enable you to live comfortably without having to sit up half the night in a smoky room.'

'Go on then,' said Morton, 'let's hear the pitch.'

'You ever come across Murgatroyd's Liniment?'

'I don't recollect that I have. What is it?'

'Why, it's the wonder of the age! It cures aching muscles, alleviates the toothache, relieves the pain of child-birth and has a thousand and one other medicinal uses besides. Made from certified rattlesnake oil, extracted fresh each day for every batch.'

'You're trying to sell me snake oil?' asked Morton in amazement. 'Get on out of here!' This time he really did leave, stalking off towards the cabins in great displeasure. The man who called himself Abernathy came after him, clutching at his sleeve.

'You got altogether the wrong idea, my friend. I'm not fixing to sell *you* the snake oil. I have a flourishing business in that field and I'm offering to exchange it for that two thousand dollars you won this evening.'

Somewhat mollified, Jack Morton suffered himself to be led back to the bar, where Abernathy bought him another drink and reasoned out the case to him.

'Here's the deal, sir. I have ashore a horse and van, fully equipped with bottles of Murgatroyd's Liniment and all the paraphernalia that goes with it. Advertising bills, bottles, labels, the whole works. Got a tame rattler as well.

You can sleep in the van, there's a bedroll, and I clear the best part of two hundred dollars a week when I'm working hard at it.

'You can do the same. Or you can fritter away that money you won tonight and be in the same position a week or two down the line. I'm offering you a way to make good money regularly, with none of the uncertainty that attends the life of a professional gambler.'

Now, although he was damned if he was going to let Abernathy see this, Morton was intrigued by this proposal. Truth to tell, he *was* growing a mite weary of sitting up half the night, playing cards and earning only enough to keep himself going. He certainly wasn't making $200 a week at this game, or anything like it.

He allowed none of this to show in his face; instead he shook his head doubtfully.

'I don't rightly know,' he said. 'I never done anything o' the kind before.

Don't you have to be a powerful slick talker for that work?'

'Not a bit of it; you just need to bluff. I've watched you do that all evening. You'd be a natural at this game.'

'I don't know,' said Jack Morton, although he was more than half-persuaded that travelling round in a horse-drawn van might make a welcome change from being on board boats, 'I wouldn't know what to say to get folks to buy the stuff.'

Sensing that he had a chance to make the sale, Abernathy said: 'Why, how right you are. I knew straight from the start that you're not a man to buy a pig in a poke. What I suggest is that you come with me to the next town and I'll show you how it's all done. Then, if you want to buy the business from me, you can do so. What do you say?'

So it was that Jack Morton let the *Delta Queen* depart without him and went on overland with Abernathy to the town of Fishers' Landing, where he was inducted into the finer points of the art of peddling snake oil to the credulous and simple-minded citizens of small Southern towns.

The first step was to announce their presence in the town; so, the evening they arrived in Fishers' Landing Morton went out with Abernathy and stuck up bills on trees and fences, letting people know that they were in town. The bills were cheaply printed but enticing. Below a lithograph of a fearsome rattler, about to strike, was printed the following message;

Cornelius Murgatroyd's Liniment

A Guaranteed Cure for Rheumatism
Whether
Acute, Chronic, Sciatic or Neuralgic
Prepared from Pure Rattlesnake Oil
Accept no Substitute and
Shun all Imitations
50c a Bottle

Relieves Instantly and Cures

Permanently; Toothache, Headache, Neuralgia, Earache, Swellings, Sprains, Stiff Joints, Sore Throats, Etc. Etc.

They scribbled on the bottom of these posters the location in town where they would be parking the van and selling their wares the next day. As they moved through Fishers' Landing, affixing these pieces of paper with thumbtacks to any convenient surface, Abernathy remarked: 'The problem with a town this small is that you can't really use shills.'

'Shills?' asked Morton. 'I don't mind that I've heard that word before. What are they?'

'Shills are men, sometimes women, that you pay to puff up your wares to the crowd,' explained Abernathy. 'You ever see the shell game, what some call 'three-card monte'?'

'Sure I have,' said Morton contemptuously. 'What has that to do with this present enterprise?'

'Ever notice how there's always

people clustered around the man running the shell game who win as easily as you like?'

'Sure, usually connections of the fellow who's actually playing with the shells or dealing the cards out. Everybody knows that. They lead on others, who will lose their money.'

'Well it's the selfsame thing in this line of work. You need to get people who buy a bottle or two at once claiming that it's cured them of the good Lord alone knows what ailments. Say, I reckon as you could play that part tomorrow. Nobody's apt to recognize you round these here parts, I dare say.'

'Happen you're right,' said Morton. 'Why do you say it's harder in little places like this?'

' 'Cause everybody knows everybody else. If I pay some fellow I picked up in a saloon the night before to praise my goods everybody'll know him at once. It's different in big towns, where you can get some fellow from the other side of the town to appear in the character of a hopeless cripple who was saved by my medicine.'

That evening Abernathy and Morton camped a little way out of town so that they wouldn't be seen together and could pose as being unknown to each other the next day. The one thing that Abernathy was not inclined to talk of was where he actually obtained his supplies of snake oil. All he would tell Morton was that he produced it himself and that it was that cheap that the only real expenses of the business were the bottles, corks, labels and suchlike; the oil itself costing next to nothing.

At nine the following morning they took the van into Fishers' Landing and set up on the patch of open land near the smithy that they had specified in the bills they had posted the previous day.

There is little enough to divert the attention in many small towns, and often curious crowds tend to gather for the most trifling of reasons. So it proved that morning, when Abernathy stood on the buckboard of his van and began his pitch.

'Ladies and gentlemen,' he said, 'you all know me. I am none other than Professor Cornelius Murgatroyd and I am, once again, passing through this fair corner of your lovely state. Some of you might ask: how come this fellow does not have a shop of his own? How is it that he does not employ agents and salesmen, or pay a small fortune to advertise his products in the newspapers?

'I'll tell you why, friends. Every batch of my snake-oil liniment is mixed up fresh, a day or two before I arrive in any town. The active ingredients of that oil degrade swiftly and, after a month in the bottle, lose their potency to an alarming degree.

'That's why I prepare my liniment just before I bottle and sell it, which is why it would be no earthly use sending it to big stores. Why, it might linger on the shelf for months and would be useless by the time it was bought.'

From the crowd gathered around the van a young man called out: 'Rattlesnake oil? You can bet it's nothing o' the sort. Rattlesnakes! I don't think so.'

'Ah,' said Abernathy, not in the smallest degree put out of countenance, 'a doubting Thomas! Come up here to the front, my friend. It's a fair point that you make and I hope to answer it.'

The man showed a marked reluctance to step forward and so Abernathy observed amiably: 'I'm sorry to note that you're afraid to set yourself openly in front of these good people and express your suspicions outright, like a man.' He made as though to continue with his spiel but the man who had sneered at the notion of rattlesnakes began pushing his way to the front, muttering: 'Afraid, am I? I don't think so. We'll see who's afraid.'

Although Morton was standing at the back of the throng surrounding Abernathy's van he was close enough to be able to tell that the salesman was not displeased to be challenged in this way.

Indeed, it was almost as though he had been expecting heckling in some form or another.

'Come on up here with me, my friend,' said Abernethy. 'Glad to see that you're not shy.' He reached down and helped the young man up on to the buckboard, saying: 'Now, you were taking leave to question as to the inclusion of genuine rattlesnakes in the medicinal product which I am this day selling. Would that about do justice to your position, sir?'

The man looked out at where his friends were standing and grinned at them. They grinned right back, thinking what a card Jim Bannister was. Then he said boldly: 'Yeah, I reckon that's about the strength of it.'

'Well then . . . I didn't catch your name?'

'M'friends call me Jim.'

'I hope I may be counted among that happy band. Just stand there a moment, Jim. I have something you might wish to see.'

Abernathy reached into the van and fumbled around for a second or two before emerging into the sun holding the biggest diamondback rattlesnake that Morton had ever seen in his life. It had to be fully four feet long. The snake-oil salesman thrust this at the young man standing beside him, saying: 'Here now, Jim, catch ahold of this!'

The results of this unexpected manoeuvre surpassed Abernathy's wildest hopes, because young Jim leaped back in terror, forgot that he was balanced precariously on a buckboard and went crashing to the earth with a loud thud. He lay there dazed, giving Abernathy the opportunity to lean over the side and enquire solicitously:

'You all right down there, Jim? Sorry to scare you like that. Didn't you say something about no rattlesnakes being used in my liniment? Still of the same opinion?'

The audience had roared with laughter to see Jim Bannister tumble to

16

the ground and they laughed anew with every word that Abernathy now spoke. Why bother hiring shills, thought that individual to himself, when there's no shortage of natural-born fools willing to play the part for free?

Waving the rattler above his head, Abernathy said loudly: 'Anybody else think that there's no rattlesnakes connected with the oil here?'

He put the snake back in the van and brought out a small piece of machinery, which looked to Jack Morton like a mincer; the sort of thing you might find clamped to a kitchen table and used for grinding sausage meat.

'I'll warrant you've all seen one of these,' said Abernathy. 'I'm going to secure it to the seat here and put this glass jar under it, so.' He matched the action to the words, then reached back into the van a final time and brought out another rattler. This one was considerably smaller than the first and not as lively. In fact it gave every sign of being stone dead.

'Now, all I do next is grind up this snake, just so.'

Along with the others, Jack Morton watched in horrified fascination as the dead snake was reduced to a slimy red pulp.

'This is only the first stage,' explained Abernathy. 'Next I have to distil this in order to extract the oil. It's a long and complicated process. But I have some bottles of the genuine article that I decanted just twelve hours ago and is as fresh and efficacious as you could wish for. Just fifty cents per bottle, and I give you my personal guarantee that if this liniment does not exceed your most extravagant expectations, why then I shall refund your money with no questions asked. Now, who's first?'

This was Morton's cue and he at once called out: 'I'll have four bottles, Professor Murgatroyd. I tell you now, I was all but crippled by my wound that I acquired in the late war and I could scarcely move a step. The doctors despaired of me and my family were resigned to looking after me for the rest of my days.

'After a week of treatment with this liniment I was able to stand, and within a month I was walking again. I bless the day I found Murgatroyd's rattlesnake oil.' After this ringing endorsement Morton bounded up to the front and handed over two dollars, receiving in exchange four bottles of the liniment.

Whether it was Jack Morton's testimonial or just that the crowd had been put into a good humour by watching young Jim Bannister make such a fool of himself, there was a brisk demand for Abernathy's wonderful elixir. They stayed all day in Fishers' Landing and by nightfall, when they harnessed up the van and were back on the road, fifty-eight bottles of snake oil had been disposed of.

'There,' said Abernathy as they rattled along the track leading away from the town. 'Twenty-nine dollars for a short day's work. What do you say to that? You'd earn a dollar a day as a cowboy. I think I've proved my point. Now, what do you say? Two thousand dollars for the whole caboodle?'

'And you'll let me in on the secret of making the stuff? It sounded kind of complicated from what you said back in Fishers' Landing.'

'Complicated? Oh, you mean touching upon boiling up rattlesnakes and such? That's only for the rubes. Here, reach me out that jar.'

'What, the one with that ground-up rattler?'

'That's the one.'

When Morton handed him the glass jar Abernathy astonished him by upending it and tipping the disgusting contents out into the road.

'You got something to learn,' Abernathy said, seeing Morton's look. 'Snake oil's got nothing at all to do with snakes. That's all part of the show.'

2

Professor Murgatroyd's rattlesnake oil proved to be a mixture of turpentine, mineral oil, beef fat and red pepper. According to Abernathy it cost no more than a couple of cents a bottle if you brought the ingredients by bulk, as he advised Morton to do. At Abernathy's urging Morton rubbed a little on his arm and felt a distinct warming sensation.

'That's the pepper,' Abernathy said when he mentioned this. 'It's the same as you get in liniment for rubbing down horses. Who knows, it might even help some poor soul suffering from the rheumatics.'

'So why pretend it's got snake oil in it?' asked Morton curiously. 'Couldn't you just tell folk the truth?'

'You think they'd rush to buy bottles of ordinary camphor, the way you saw them do today? The show is what makes them think they're getting something mysterious, with unknown powers. I'm telling you for now, they wouldn't shell out fifty cents a bottle for camphor with a dash of pepper.'

'Why snakes, though? That's the bit I don't get.'

'It started with the coolies. They really did use to make stuff from snakes. They did it back home in China and then, when they came over here, they tried making the same concoction. Everybody thought it sounded grand and so now people expect to find snake oil in their medicines. It doesn't do any harm to believe it.'

The next day Jack Morton and Abernathy parted company on good terms after $2,000 had changed hands. With a few final tips on keeping the tame rattler harmless and how to catch the snakes needed for the show, Abernathy went off and Morton never saw him again.

He never did learn what it was that

the man had needed all that money for, nor why he'd suddenly given up the snake oil business.

★ ★ ★

So, a year and a half down the line, Jack Morton, also known as Professor Cornelius Murgatroyd, was carrying on the trade of snake oil merchant and, by and large, finding it to be a satisfying and financially rewarding undertaking. Just as Abernathy had promised, in a good week he could net $200 and, because his living expenses were low, Morton found himself able to save a little. It was a vast improvement on the hand-to-mouth existence that he'd led on the riverboats.

One refinement that Morton had added to his persona as Professor Cornelius Murgatroyd was to grow a neat little goatee, which gave him something of the look of a youthful Jefferson Davis. He had invested, too, in an elegant white linen suit. Though he said it himself, Jack Morton felt that he had improved in no small measure upon the act that he had inherited from Abernathy.

Although he had no overall plan of campaign in mind, Morton had over the last year been heading further and further west. After taking on the snake oil business he had travelled through Mississippi, Louisiana and Arkansas. Now, he had moved into northern Texas and was vaguely moving towards New Mexico. The towns in Texas were further apart than down on the Louisiana coast, but then again, the further west he travelled, the fewer competitors he encountered.

He had heard tales in Arkansas of rival snake oil salesmen coming to blows over those who encroached upon what they saw as their territory. In one incident, a van and all the stock contained in it had been wantonly burned and the owner put out of business permanently. There didn't look to be anything of that nature in Texas:

at least as far as Morton had seen so far.

The next town along the road was called Endurance. From what Morton could gather around 2,000 souls lived there. There was probably no chance of using shills, so he would be forced to rely entirely upon his own blandishments. Well, that was fine; it wasn't the first time and would be unlikely to be the last.

As was his custom Jack Morton halted his van some half a mile from the town and scanned the place carefully. It didn't look too prosperous, but that needn't necessarily be a bad sign. Sometimes poor people were more gullible and easily tricked out of their money than the shrewd and well-to-do. In fact, it was those who were hard up and ill-educated who were often most eager to believe the tales that he spun about the wonderful properties of his rattlesnake oil. These were people who could not, in general, afford to pay a doctor and so were dependent upon patent medicines like his if their child fell ill or they themselves developed some physical affliction that interfered with their lives. Yes, he had high hopes for Endurance.

The trouble started next day, almost as soon as he began his spiel. The most annoying and ridiculous aspect of the thing was that it all had nothing at all to do with him, notwithstanding the fact that it almost cost him his life.

There was a bunch of especially rough cowboys in town, evidently hell-bent on raising Cain. Why, he didn't know. Howsoever, the sight of many of the townsfolk gathered around his van acted like a magnet. These men from out of town came up behind those listening to Morton and began jostling and shoving. Nor did they restrict their attentions to the men; in next to no time there was pandemonium when the accusation was made that somebody's wife had been assaulted. The affronted husband drew on the cowboy who, he said, had taken this liberty; then, unbelievably, the shooting began.

Morton was used to hearing occasional gunfire late at night, when drunken men would make whoopee by shooting out somebody's window or even firing at another drunk who had insulted them. But this was ten in the morning!

There were three or four shots, then a pause as his audience scattered and sought cover: either diving to the ground or hiding behind trees. Then there was a final crack, which echoed back and forth between the nearby buildings. No sooner had he heard it than Jack Morton felt a sharp pain in his side and realized in amazement that he had been shot.

'Ah, shit!' he muttered, then sat down at once on the driving seat of the van.

Morton tried to calm down and slow the frantic beating of his heart. He knew that terror causes the heart to pump faster and the blood to flow more freely from a wound. It was important to find out how badly he was hurt.

The pain was in his left side, on the ribs, right where his heart was situated. Fearfully he removed his jacket and saw that a ragged hole had been torn through it at the breast. Then he looked down and saw the slowly spreading crimson stain.

He unbuttoned his vest and removed it, discovering as he did so that that too had a neat round hole in the left-hand side. Despite his efforts to remain calm, Morton was aware of his heart pounding and the blood singing in his ears.

He was now ready to examine the wound itself. Slowly, he unbuttoned the shirt and moved it aside. Looking down, he could see that a long, narrow groove had been gouged across his ribs. He took a huge gulp of air in relief and immediately felt a stabbing pain in his side. Presumably the ball had cracked one of his ribs. But that was all right: he could live with that.

It was an awkward and undignified

procedure, stripping to the waist in public and checking himself for mortal wounds, but there it was. He wasn't going to die of a little embarrassment. If he bound up that rib tight, he would do well enough. It wasn't the first of his ribs to be broken and he knew what to expect. The ball must have gone through his clothing and then caught him a glancing blow, skidding off the rib, its force being dissipated in that way. A fraction of an inch to one side and it would have driven straight into his heart. There could hardly have been a narrower escape.

Now that he knew that he would live Jack Morton was more vexed by the damage to his white linen suit than he was by the injury to his rib. That suit had cost him plenty and he was grieved to see it ruined. Sure, he had some rough work clothes in the back of the van, but that white suit was part of the act; it conjured up Professor Cornelius Murgatroyd and brought him to life. He would have to replace the clothing as soon as he was able.

Having established to his own satisfaction that he was not about to expire on the spot, Morton began to take an interest once again in the terrestrial scheme of things. He saw, and not with any great surprise, that judgment was about to be executed upon one of the cowboys who had disturbed his sales pitch.

A thing that Jack Morton had noticed over the years was that people like him: drifters and ne'er-do-wells, habitually underestimated the passions of those who lived settled and orderly lives. In his more whimsical moments, Morton liked to think of himself as a predator, preying upon the vulnerable folk who lived in these little hick towns: a wolf, moving among sheep. Others felt the same way about the citizens of burgs like Endurance. Probably those cowboys had much the same view of the matter, thinking that they could push people around and generally act like they owned the place.

Every once in a while though, characters like Morton and the cowboys would learn the hard way that the men living in and around out-of-the-way towns and hamlets were just the same as them, really. Specifically, they could be every bit as hard and ruthless. As he pulled his shirt back on it looked to Morton as though the men, who had a few minutes earlier been prospective customers of his, were now engaged in settling a score in the most brutal and direct manner imaginable.

There were only a half-dozen of those cowboys, for all that they had been making so much of themselves. Now that it was plain that they were so vastly outnumbered by the men of Endurance they had stopped their blustering and were trying to slip away without any fuss. The only thing, there was a man lying dead on the ground, shot through the head. He was somebody who had been known to all those living in the town, and it looked to Morton as though the dead man's friends and neighbours were determined that there should be a reckoning for this pointless killing.

Fascinated, despite the repugnance he felt at what he guessed would be the final outcome, Morton jumped down from the buckboard and joined the throng of angry men and women who were now surrounding the cowboys who had provoked the bloody confrontation. The men in the crowd had all drawn their guns and it must have been plain to the cowboys who now faced the wrath of the town that there was little chance of breaking free by main force, so they were adopting a pacific attitude, designed to placate the anger of the crowd.

'Hey, sorry about that, but he drew on us. We didn't start it,' said one man. Another tried unobtrusively to detach himself from his fellows and get free. He was detected in this attempt and shepherded back to the other five.

There were further protestations of regret, innocence and sorrow at the outcome of the little bit of friction that had erupted. Nothing, however, could explain or excuse the dead man lying there in the road; Morton was sure in his own mind that there would swiftly be a deadly reckoning for this.

He was right.

Endurance, like so many small towns at that time, did not have a sheriff, relying instead upon the services of a vigilance committee, which kept order in and around the town. Word was sent to the head of this committee, who was working over on the other side of town. When he arrived it was obvious that he took a very dim view of fatal shootings on the streets of the town, which he had pledged himself to keep safe for decent people.

'Who started this?' asked Terrance Drake, whose regular job was running the livery stable. 'Let's hear from those as live here first.' There was a clamour of protest from the six cowboys.

'You boys'll get your turn later,' Drake told them.

'Those fellows were pushing and shoving at us while we was watching the show over yonder,' said one man. 'It was them as started the trouble.'

'Show?' asked Terrance Drake. 'What show would this be?' Somebody pointed to Morton's van with its gaudily painted advertisement emblazoned on the side.

'Oh,' said Drake. 'Snake oil man in town, is there? Where might I see that gentleman?'

Jack Morton was not all that keen on drawing attention to himself, but some members of the crowd pointed him out. The leader of the vigilance committee eyed him coldly.

'We don't encourage men like you in this town,' he said. 'I'll speak a word or two to you later.' Then he turned his attention back to the shooting. 'You Tom, and you too, Patrick,' he said to men nearby, 'bring me the pistols of those men, one at a time.'

When the first gun was brought to

him Drake sniffed delicately at the barrel.

'This 'un ain't been fired lately,' he announced. 'Whose gun is this?' When the owner was identified Drake said: 'Put him to one side.' He repeated the process with all the pistols, finding that only two had been fired recently.

Morton was struck with admiration for the fair way that the investigation was being conducted so far. There were towns where those men might just have been beaten up so badly that some of them died. Here there was at least the semblance of justice, albeit of a rough and ready variety.

Having found that one or other of the two men had been responsible for killing a man known to him, who had lived peaceably in the town for many years, Terrence Drake was not minded to waste too many words on the affair. He addressed the two cowboys thus: 'I don't enquire into who drew first, nor anything of that kind. It's plain from what's been said that you boys came causing trouble today and that's on your own heads. From all that I am able to collect, one of you touched the dead man's wife in a lewd way and, like any decent husband, he was angry. Only thing I want to know now is, which of you killed him?'

Neither of the accused men seemed disposed towards making a confession, so Drake concluded by saying: 'I don't much care if we hang one or both of you. You can argue the case out between yourselves for . . . ' he glanced up at the clock on the church, 'ten minutes. If after that time you're both obstinate, then you hang together. Some of you take them over to the store there and let them talk. Make sure, though, as they don't escape.'

Although he didn't really care for such spectacles, Morton found that he was unable to tear himself away and go about his business. All other consider-ations apart, he wanted to see if the murderer would own up in order to spare his partner from also being hanged. He'd never come across such a strange situation before and the very novelty of the thing kept him rooted to the spot.

After ten minutes the two cowboys were brought out of the store and thrust before Terrance Drake, who stood there like some Old Testament prophet about to call down the wrath of God.

'Well?' he asked. 'Either o' you two got anything to say?'

'It was me that shot him,' mumbled one of the two men. 'But he drew on me first. It was self-defence.'

'Nobody cares a damn about that. You started the trouble, interfering with a man's wife. You had your fun, now it's time to pay for it.' Drake called over to somebody standing near the store. 'Tom, you know what to do.'

Right up until this moment Morton had had the impression that neither of the two cowboys really thought that they were in peril of their lives. Perhaps they thought that the aim was to give them a shock, warn them off and get them to leave town at once.

After all, if the man who had admitted the killing was telling the truth and the dead man had drawn on him, then by all the rules of fair play that Jack Morton had ever heard tell of it was indeed a case of self-defence. Maybe they would just knock the fellow about a bit before sending the six troublemakers on their way.

That was the way that Morton's thoughts were tending and evidently the killer too had been reasoning along those same lines, because when he saw the man, Tom, emerge from the store with a coil of rope in his hand he made a bolt for it, all of a sudden apprehending that his very life was now to be forfeited for a moment's wildness.

'I don't know your name and to speak plainly, I don't much care what it is,' Drake told the cowboy, who, after his attempt at running, was now being grasped firmly by three or four stalwart men. 'In this town, you kill a man, you pay with your life.' He turned to the men holding the condemned killer. 'Hang him,' he said.

As he was being dragged across the dusty street to where an oak spread its branches outside the forge, the cowboy tried to dig his heels into the ground like a mule. The scene sickened Jack Morton, who was put in mind of a beast being taken to slaughter. As the struggling group came closer to the fatal tree the man redoubled his efforts to break free and then began screaming in terror.

A noose had already been fashioned and slung over a branch. Somehow or other, in spite of his frantic endeavours, the man's hands were lashed behind him with a rawhide thong and the noose placed around his neck. There was little point in prolonging matters; as soon as the rope was secure willing hands took hold of the other end and hauled the man into the air. It was a mercifully swift death, with the victim's kicks ending after only a minute or less.

It had been a grim enough business, but as fairly and equitably conducted as anything of that type that Morton had witnessed before. He was wondering what would be a decent interval to let elapse before resuming his pitch when a man came up to him.

'Mr Drake begs the favour of a word,' he said.

The man who had just ordered a man's hanging looked at Jack Morton as though he had just crawled out from under some especially grubby rock.

'Snake oil, hey?' he asked, his face set and grim. 'You just seen how we keep this town wholesome and clean. I'm telling you now that we don't take to bunco artists or snake oil salesmen here in any way, shape or form.

'If you're still here in an hour, I'm going to get a few of my men to knock you about a bit and maybe smash that van of yours to matchwood. That plain enough for you?'

'I've been shot,' said Morton. 'You might have noticed.'

'You hadn't been standing up there on the buck-board, trying to gull folk out of their money for your worthless goods, the bullet wouldn't o' struck you. You have an hour.'

Having seen the utterly ruthless way in which Drake and his vigilantes handled visitors to the town of whom they disapproved, Morton did not feel in the slightest degree inclined towards staying around and seeing if the threat of violence would be put into practice. He knew damned well that Terrance Drake meant just exactly what he meant. All he could do was cut his losses and try his luck in the next town, which was a larger one than this from what he'd heard. After harnessing up the horse Jack Morton shook the dust of that place from his feet and made tracks, heading west to Oneida.

All in all, Morton thought that things could have turned out a lot worse. It was true that his suit was ruined, but then again, he was still alive. He'd been thrown out of the town, but no intentional violence had been inflicted upon him, and his stock was secure.

It wasn't the first time he'd been compelled to make a precipitate departure from a town and he figured that it would most likely not be the last either. That was what this line of work was like; some folk objected to it. He felt no animosity towards Terrance Drake. When all was said and done, the fellow was just protecting the citizens of his town from being skinned by a rogue.

Morton drove on for the day and then camped off the road for the night. He'd fed his rattler with a plump little baby jackrabbit just a couple of days before, so he didn't need to fret about hunting anything. He had enough in the van for his own needs and after a light meal he turned in for the night before it was completely dark.

3

At first light Morton woke and gathered up some dry twigs and branches so that he could boil up some coffee. He needed nothing else in the way of breakfast. There was nothing to delay him, so Morton set out before the sun had risen far above the horizon.

He had been travelling for two hours or thereabouts when he heard the crack of a rifle ahead of him. This was followed quickly by the sound of pistol fire and then another shot from a rifle or scattergun. He reined in the horse and turned round, pulling out an old army rifle that he kept for emergencies. He cocked this and placed it on the buckboard at his feet. Then he pulled out the pistol that he had usually sported before he'd gone into this line of work and tucked it in his belt. People don't as a rule expect to see a professor going heeled and so he felt it more in keeping with his persona not to pack iron while peddling his wares. But if there was going to be some lively action now, then Morton sure as hell aimed to be prepared.

The road to Oneida wove through a series of miniature canyons and gullies, making it hard to calculate how far away the shooting had been. Morton found out when he turned a corner and found himself fifty yards from what he at once took to be an attempted robbery of some kind. He reined in the horse and took stock.

A covered wagon drawn by four horses was standing in the road ahead. It was an old-looking vehicle; what would once have been described as a prairie schooner. Surrounding the wagon were two riders, both with guns in their hands. They looked round sharply when Morton's van hove into view, clearly wondering if this new arrival posed any threat to their activities. Another man had dismounted and was in the process of climbing into the back of the covered wagon.

The two riders watched Morton carefully, trying perhaps to work out if he represented any sort of threat to them. A man lay prone near by and it took no great power of thought to work out that he had been driving the wagon and that one or more of those gathered round had shot him.

As far as Jack Morton's code of ethics went, he wasn't called upon to interfere in whatever was happening ahead of him. If those men let him be, then he was happy enough to return the compliment and leave them to their own devices. He wasn't a one to go looking for trouble nor, for the matter of that, to set out and meet it halfway. Morton checked that his piece was loose in his belt and the rifle ready to pluck up, should need arise. Then he waited to see how matters would develop.

That was, until he heard the shriek of a terrified woman, which was followed almost instantly by two more shots. Much as he hated to intervene in a quarrel that was no affair of his, Morton was not about to let a woman be molested. With great reluctance he touched up his horse and carried on towards the wagon.

Something untoward had happened to the three robbers, because the man who had got into the wagon had fallen back out again and was lying on the ground, yelling in pain. His partners in crime were at a loss to know how to deal with this. One of them turned to face Morton as he drew closer.

'You know what's best for you, you're goin' to keep right on, mister,' said this man.

'Can't do that, pilgrim,' Morton replied, in a friendly enough tone. 'I heard a woman scream and I mean to know what you're about.'

What with his friend having apparently just been shot and things not going as planned, the man who had spoken to Morton was seemingly all out of patience, because he pointed his pistol straight at him.

'You hear what I tell you, you whore's son? Make tracks,' he said.

If there was one thing that Jack Morton could not abide at any price it was having men aim firearms at him. He'd had a bellyful of that in the war, and ever since the surrender he had not put up with such a thing from anybody.

Morton raised his hands defensively.

'Hell,' he said, 'there ain't no call for that, I'm going.' He fumbled with the reins, then dropped them as though he were panicking. He bent down, but instead of picking up the reins he snatched up the rifle lying there at his feet, brought it up to the mark and fired at once. The ball took the man who had been menacing Morton straight in the centre of his breast.

Without bothering to check that the man was dead Morton dropped the rifle and at once pulled out his Navy Colt, which was tucked loosely in his belt, cocking it with his thumb as he did so. He drew down on the other rider, but this man, seeing two of his comrades shot, had had enough. Jabbing his mount viciously in the flanks with his spurs he galloped off, leaving the field to Jack Morton.

The man he had shot was dead. He had toppled from the saddle and crashed to the ground. His horse was grazing placidly near by. In addition to the other dead body there was the man who had, as far as Morton was able to apprehend, been shot just before he came on to the scene. This fellow was writhing around in agony, moaning, over and over: 'She shot me, she shot me!'

Morton jumped down and checked that this man was unarmed; he had no wish to be shot in the back, unawares. Then he went over to the wagon to see what had become of the woman whom he had heard screaming.

As he pulled aside the flap at the rear of the wagon a horrible sight was revealed. A young woman lay on her back amid a heap of household goods and suchlike. It looked to Morton as though she had been moving home. Maybe she was one of those whose husband had claimed a quarter-section under the Homestead Act and they had been moving to start a new life somewhere.

Whatever her plans had been, she was not likely to be in a position to bring them to fruition now. Even without any medical knowledge at all it was not hard to see that she had lost at least a quart of blood. At a guess, thought Morton, a bullet had sliced through one of her arteries and she would be unlikely to last more than another ten minutes at best. When the woman saw Morton, she cried in a determined but weak voice: 'Come here. Quick now, I need to tell you what to do.'

For a moment, he thought that the

woman was mistaking him for somebody else, but then he knew that it wasn't that at all. She simply knew that she was dying and had something important that needed to be said before she lost consciousness. Morton hauled himself up into the wagon.

'Rest easy now,' he said to the woman, 'you're not alone.'

'No time for that. Over there — in the box — it's Robert. After Robert E. Lee, you know.'

'Don't fret about that,' Morton said soothingly, thinking that she was wandering in her mind. 'Just lie easy now.'

'No,' she said fiercely. 'Fetch him. Fetch Robert.'

To humour her Morton crawled over to where she indicated, in the corner. Then he received something of a shock. For there, nestling within a wooden crate, was a baby.

'Lord a mercy!' said Morton, appalled at the thought that this helpless morsel of humanity was likely to be orphaned in another few minutes. He picked up the child, who was swaddled up in a blanket, and took him to the woman, who, he guessed, must be the mother. He handed the baby to her.

'Here you are, ma'am,' he said.

The woman took the child in her arms.

'There, little one,' she murmured. 'I have to go soon.' Her breathing was shallow and rapid. Morton knew the signs; he had seen men suffering so on the battlefield. This woman was very close to the end.

'Listen to me,' she said. 'Promise to take my baby to Claremont.'

'Where? I don't understand.'

'Claremont. It's a town not far from here. My father is there. Martin Catchpole. Take my baby to him. He'll know what's best.'

'What happened?' asked Morton.

'Those men jumped us. They shot Brent. Then they looked in here and I shot one of them. He shot me. Take Robert to my father. Promise me.'

'I'll do it. Is there anything I can do to make you more comfortable?'

'I'm dying. It doesn't matter. Look after my baby.'

The woman closed her eyes and her breathing grew ragged. It was impossible to imagine that a human body contained so much blood. It soaked her dress and was pooling on the wooden floor of the wagon. This too was something that Morton recalled vividly from the war; that when once an artery was nicked the sheer quantity of blood was always far more than you'd expect.

As Morton watched helplessly the unknown woman gave a convulsive gulp, breathed in deeply and then let the air out, until her lungs were quite empty. She didn't draw breath again and, as if it sensed what had happened, the infant began screaming inconsolably.

For a minute, Jack Morton squatted there, overcome with horror at witnessing the death of a young mother and the orphaning of her child. Then he recollected the wounded man whom he'd left outside and his wrath rose up, choking him. He had an intense hatred for those who harmed the weak and helpless and there were no words strong enough to condemn a man who would shoot a woman dead.

He jumped down from the wagon and went over to where the man who had been moaning about having been shot by a woman had been rolling about in agony. It had been Morton's aim to put a bullet through this villain's head with no more ado, but he found that he was too late. The man was already dead.

Looking around him now Morton could see three dead men. He shook his head and muttered to himself: 'This is the devil of a business!' The baby, young Robert, was still wailing with grief, hunger or the Lord knew what else. The full implications of the situation began to sink home and Morton wondered what on earth he was going to do. He had never in the whole course of his life so much as picked up or held a baby. How the hell was he supposed to take this one an unknown distance to some town and then find his grandfather? Why, it wasn't to be thought of!

The keening cry of the baby was getting on Morton's nerves and he knew that he would have to do something about it. All else apart, he could hardly leave the living child for much longer, locked in the embrace of a corpse. Although he was the least superstitious and squeamish of men he shuddered at the thought.

The squalling infant quietened as he saw Morton climb back into the wagon. His eyes followed the man and then widened in pleasure as he was picked up.

'Well fella,' Morton said, 'you and me're going to be travelling together for a space and the Lord only knows how that's going to pan out. Tell me now, what sort o' vittles do children of your age thrive on?'

Morton hadn't expected, nor did he receive, an answer to his question. Raking through the belongings stowed in the wagon brought to light two jars containing a mushy and unappetizing mess of what looked to be some sort of porridge. He found a spoon and dipped it into this disgusting substance. The baby — he supposed that he really should start thinking of him as 'Robert' — took to the mush with relish and Morton carried him awkwardly out into the fresh air. It didn't somehow seem right to be feeding this little one in the presence of his own dead mother.

The baby wolfed down a considerable quantity of the food, which Morton devoutly hoped was wholesome for it, then it stopped; a thoughtful look came upon its chubby little face.

'You all right there?' asked Morton. He brought the child up to examine it more closely, whereupon it vomited up over the front of Morton's shirt.

'Ah, shit!' he exclaimed. 'That's all I need.'

Since his fetching up in the little town of Endurance, it had to be said that Jack Morton's appearance had deteriorated sharply. It was hard to see, in the dishevelled figure squatting by that dusty track, the dapper and elegantly turned out Professor Cornelius Murgatroyd. The shirt he was wearing was torn and bloodstained by the injury that he had received to his rib, the pain of which had scarcely abated. Now, he had gobbets of partially digested food dripping down his shirtfront as well.

Well accustomed as he was to the repartee of the audiences that he faced, Morton could only too well imagine the jeers that would greet him if he tried to peddle his snake oil while showing evidence of an injury like this. He could almost hear the cries of: 'Is your medicine any good for bullet wounds, Professor?' and the gales of laughter that would greet such a sally.

It was the irritation of having the baby sick up over him that first put into

Morton's mind the idea of disregarding the vow he had made to the dying woman and, instead, trying to offload this baby on to somebody else at the first opportunity. His conscience was by no means a tender organ and he felt that he had been rather buffaloed into making that promise to undertake a journey of unknown length and duration in order to deliver a child that was no concern of his to somebody to whom he owed nothing at all.

Oh, he wouldn't just abandon the child by the roadside; he wasn't such a cur as that, but he was damned if he wouldn't find somebody else who might wish to care for the brat and fulfil the woman's dying wishes.

His rib was throbbing from the exertion of hopping in and out of the wagon, and this didn't perhaps make Jack Morton's temper any the sweeter. He laid the baby on the ground and climbed back into the wagon, averting his gaze from the dead woman, who presented a ghastly aspect. Near the box in which the baby had been placed for a cradle he found a bunch of clothing, including what he supposed were diapers. There was also powdered grain, which Morton thought would need to be mixed up with water, along with a flagon of milk.

Before he clambered down again it struck Morton that maybe he should say a prayer or something for the bloody corpse who until a matter of minutes ago had been a living, breathing human person. As always, he felt a sense of awe when in the presence of death, mingled with an uncomfortable sense of his own mortality.

'I'll make sure to take your baby to those as are best able to take care of it — I mean him,' he said aloud. 'I'm not really the man for the job, but I make no doubt that there'll be somebody in that town I'm heading for, will be able to do the job a sight better than I am able.

'I hope that the Lord takes care of you and all, that you are in heaven and so on.' Morton didn't know if he should conclude this brief statement with 'Amen' and decided in the end to omit it. There was a limit even to the hypocrisy of a snake oil merchant.

Outside the wagon the baby was starting to grizzle again, so Morton stepped down, carrying all the clothes and other bits and pieces. He stowed these in the back of his van, then went back and picked up the baby, who seemed to be comforted by the contact with another human body. With the infant seated on his lap, and holding the reins in one hand, he set off for Oneida.

Although it took only two hours to reach the town the journey seemed to Morton to last a good deal longer than that. This was because the baby on his lap kept up a more or less continuous caterwauling, which went right through Morton's head. He was not sorry eventually to see scattered farms and then closely packed houses, which told him that he was approaching a substantial town.

There, on the very edge of the town, stood the answer to Jack Morton's prayers. A grim-looking building surrounded by high railings announced itself on a board at the entrance to be the Oneida Orphans' Asylum. 'If this ain't what's needful,' muttered Morton to himself, 'I surely don't know what is!' He reined in the horse and climbed down from the buckboard.

Jack Morton's conscience wasn't altogether clear about fobbing the helpless infant off on to somebody else. At the back of his mind he knew fine well that he had promised the dying woman in that wagon that he would himself undertake to care for her baby and take it to the town of Claremont; Morton's morality, however, was flexible enough for him to believe that he would still be fulfilling this vow if he only found others to engage to take on the task. If he left the child in this here orphans' asylum and gave them the name of the dead woman's kin, then wouldn't they deal with the matter at least as well as he might himself have done? Whether or no, that was what he planned to do.

The wrought iron gate to the establishment was seven feet tall and topped with sharp spikes. Morton rang the bell pull set into the cement pillar supporting the gate. Nothing had happened after two minutes so he tried again. A thin, washed-out looking little boy emerged from a side door and wandered listlessly over to where Morton stood, holding the baby awkwardly.

'You took your time,' Morton observed sharply.

'Just let me in, will you?'

The boy shrugged. 'Gate's locked.' He made no effort either to leave or to make any attempt to see about having the gate unlocked.

'Just look lively, will you, son, and fetch somebody as'll open it up. Come on, I don't have all day.'

The child, who looked to be about ten years of age, retreated into the house. After another long wait a stern-faced woman in her middle years appeared and asked what Morton wanted.

'I've a baby here, as you can see,' he replied. 'It's an orphan and this here's an orphanage and I thought the two circumstances went together.'

The woman was wearing an iron chatelaine about her waist and she selected a key from this with which to open the gate. Having done so she stepped aside. Taking this as an invitation Morton stepped forward; the woman at once locked the gate behind him.

'You keeping intruders out or locking the children in?' he enquired, to which the woman made no answer.

Morton followed the silent woman along the path to the building, which put him in mind more of a penitentiary than anything else he could call to mind. There were a number of pale, listless-looking children to be seen in the corridors, all engaged in domestic tasks such as cleaning and polishing. There was something indefinably and yet undeniably unwholesome about the atmosphere of the place and for the first time in some years Morton's conscience awoke and clamoured for attention.

He knew then that he could not possibly abandon the baby he held in arms to this grim and forbidding institution. He stopped dead in his tracks. The woman looked back at him quizzically.

'I'm right sorry to have wasted your time, ma'am,' he told her, 'but I suddenly recollect that I have some business to attend to. I'll have to trouble you to let me out again.'

'I thought you wanted rid of that child.'

'The truth is, I've taken a wrong turn somewhere. Just unlock the gate, will you, and I'll be vastly obliged to you for the favour.'

For a moment or two Morton honestly thought that the woman was going to refuse his request, that he might find himself imprisoned within this ghastly building and forbidden to leave. Then, with an ill grace, the woman turned back and retraced her steps to the entrance of the grounds, with Morton trailing after her. Wordlessly she unlocked the gate and, with a feeling of enormous relief, Morton hurried out on to the sidewalk. He heard the click of the lock turning behind him; when he glanced back it was to see the fearsome woman disappearing back into the orphanage.

4

'You're a damned fool, Morton,' he muttered to himself irritably. 'You could o' be shot o' this wretched child by now, had you the sense God gave a goat.'

There came a discreet cough. Morton turned to find a sober-looking individual standing behind him. The man was clad entirely in black and was perhaps forty years of age. He had about him an unworldly and pious air, which caused Morton to suspect that he might be a preacher of some kind. This proved to be the case, because the man stretched forth his hand, saying: 'The Reverend Habakkuk Jefferson at your service, sir.'

They shook and Morton replied: 'Glad to know you Reverend. Is there something I can do for you?'

'To speak plainly, my son, it may be

so. I am pastor at the Oneida Full Gospel Redemption Tabernacle Church. Perhaps you have heard of us?'

'I'm afraid I'm new to these parts. Besides which, I'm not a great one for churchgoing, so one church is much the same as another to me. How can I help you?'

The Reverend Jefferson stepped a little closer to Morton and lowered his voice a fraction.

'I could not help but observe that you are a travelling purveyor of snake oil liniment. Is that correct?'

'Why yes. Can I sell you a bottle or two?'

The Reverend Jefferson smiled and shook his head.

'No, we in my church put our faith in the Lord when we are afflicted with any bodily infirmities. Tell me, though, men of your profession oft times carry along of you a rattlesnake or two. By which I mean living snakes, which you exhibit to those whom you would impress with the efficacy of the medicine that you would have them purchase. Is that the case with you?'

'You mean have I a tame rattler in back of my van? Yes, I do. What of it?'

The minister was staring at Morton; he said abruptly: 'You look to have been in the wars, sir. I notice that you have been bleeding. Would you like to break bread with my wife and myself? We are God-fearing folk; you need have no apprehensions. Perhaps we might do each other a favour?'

Jack Morton looked down at his soiled and filthy shirt; the bullet hole was plainly visible and fringed with bloodstains. The idea of resting up somewhere and having a bite to eat was an attractive one.

'You want to hop up here with me and direct us to your home?' he said.

Reverend Jefferson looked shocked at the very notion.

'That wouldn't do at all. As the poet said: 'Who shall escape calumny?' There are those who would think the worse of me if I were seen in the company of a man pursuing your occupation. Not that I share this prejudice, you understand, but a man in my position has to be extra specially careful about not giving those with evil tongues an opportunity to spread malicious gossip.'

'What do you suggest?'

'We live over on the other side of town. Here, let me write down our address. I beg you not to bring your vehicle by the house, that wouldn't do at all. But when you've made provision, then you and the child can come and see us.'

It was apparent to Morton that this gentleman of the cloth was restless and did not wish to prolong the conversation in public. When Habakkuk Jefferson had gone off about his own affairs Morton wondered to himself what the blazes this could be about. What the devil could a clergyman be wanting with a tame rattlesnake? Well, doubtless he would soon learn.

It wasn't too difficult to find a livery

stable where the horse could be turned out and the van left in a barn. By a great mercy Morton had been able to save a fair amount each week and was consequently pretty flush just then. He wondered what to do about the snake, but decided that it would do no harm to leave it in the tea chest, at least until he knew what Reverend Jefferson wanted with it. He bundled young Robert's clothes and food into a bag, which he slung across his shoulders, then made for the address that he had been given.

'Come in my friend, come in,' said Jefferson when he opened the door to Morton and his young charge. 'You are both very welcome.'

There was a meal waiting on the table, for which Jack Morton was thankful. He had rather neglected his belly over the last few days, what with one thing and another. Mrs Jefferson was an agreeable woman who was happy to take hold of Robert. When she did so, her nose wrinkled.

'Forgive my being so blunt, Mr Morton,' she said, 'but when was this child's diaper last changed?'

'I wouldn't know ma'am. Not since I took charge of him, some hours since.'

'I meant to ask you,' said the Reverend Jefferson. 'How do you come to be looking after a child of such tender years? I make no doubt that there is a curious tale behind the circumstance. You do not, if you will not take my saying so amiss, strike me as a man who has had much dealings with babies.'

'It's by way of being a long story. If your wife would instruct me in the art of changing a diaper it would be a kindness on her part.'

'There's nothing to it at all,' said Mrs Jefferson. 'Here, let me show you now.'

For the next half-hour, Morton was introduced to the feminine mysteries of caring for a helpless baby; he proved a willing student. At last, with her husband growing impatient to eat, there was a break in the lesson and the three adults seated themselves at the table. After a long and flowery grace was said, they began eating.

Morton thought it time to discover what use a minister might have for a rattlesnake and he asked outright what it was all about. He was grateful for the meal and even more grateful for having had one or two matters relating to the care of babies explained to him; he thought that he owed a favour in return.

'Do you read scripture much, Mr Morton?' asked the Reverend Jefferson.

'Can't say as I do.'

'So you might not be familiar with Mark, sixteen, verse eighteen: 'they shall take up serpents; and if they drink any deadly thing, it shall not hurt them; they shall lay hands on the sick, and they shall recover.'?'

A light dawned upon Morton and he saw where all this was tending.

'You're one o' those snake-handling pastors I hear tell of?'

'That is precisely right. Only, before I

71

handle serpents I like to make sure what I'm about. Tell me, has your snake been fed lately? Not hungry and irritable, I suppose?'

'Not a bit of it,' said Morton, 'and I'm guessing that the next question is likely to be: when did I last milk it?'

'You anticipate me sir,' said Jefferson, smiling broadly. 'I see we understand each other very well.'

'Milking a snake?' asked Mrs Jefferson. 'I never heard of such a thing. What can the two of you be talking about?'

'It's an expression we use ma'am,' explained Morton. 'I wouldn't want to handle a rattler, even a tame one, without making sure that there's little venom in his fangs. So every few days I hold it and annoy it 'til it's ready to strike. Then I make sure that it sinks its teeth into a piece of parchment stretched over the mouth of a jar. The venom sprays out and it takes a while for the rattler to make a new lot.'

'Well I declare, I never heard the like!'

'You may not have done, ma'am, but your husband here isn't a man who wishes to take needless chances.'

'I trust in scripture,' said Reverend Jefferson, 'but the Lord wants us to take ordinary precautions as well.'

'You're welcome enough to use my snake in your show,' said Morton. Then a thought struck him. 'Say, would you like me to attend your church and offer up a testimonial or something? Strikes me that the two of us are in the same line of business in a way.'

'You are very welcome to worship the Lord with us tonight,' said the minister, a little stiffly. Morton had the idea that he might have been offended to be compared with a man in Morton's business.

While they talked and ate little Robert was grizzling in the background more or less constantly. The noise grated on Jack Morton's nerves and he asked Mrs Jefferson: 'Say, do you know why he's making that noise all the time? You think he's hungry, thirsty, tired or what?'

'Bless you, he's teething. All babies are fussy at that time.'

As he strolled down to the livery stable to pick up his snake for Jefferson to use in what he thought of as just another show, Morton turned over in his mind what he knew of the snake handlers. There had been a congregation of such people in Tennessee a few years earlier, who had picked up during their services all manner of venomous snakes. Being faithful servants of the Lord had not prevented two or three of them dying after being bitten.

That was as nothing though, to what happened when they moved on from 'holding serpents' to drinking 'any deadly thing', which, according to the Bible, 'would not hurt them'. The veracity of this claim had been tested to the limit when seven men, women and children had died agonizingly of strychnine poisoning. The sensible ones who wished to work that dodge now did what the Reverend Jefferson did and obtained their serpents from a reliable source.

It was awkward, carrying the tea chest across to the Jeffersons' place, but Morton was a fellow who believed in paying his debts. It could not be denied that Mrs Jefferson had given him some right good counsel regarding the care of the baby and he'd a notion that she would be happy to pass on a few more tips before he headed north towards Claremont.

The baby was as quiet as anything, lying on his back, drowsily. The minister's wife was sitting placidly near at hand, doing some sewing and mending.

'Why ma'am,' said Morton, 'you have a way with children, I can see. That's the most restful I've seen the boy. You must show me what you do.'

Reverend Jefferson interrupted at this point.

'We can investigate the finer points of

child-rearing later. Perhaps you would show me this snake of yours?'

Morton set the tea chest on the floor, prised off the lid and lifted out the rattlesnake.

'My,' said the minister, 'that's a fine specimen! You're sure it's had the venom drawn lately?'

'As much as is possible. If it were to bite you, you might suffer as much as if a hornet had stung you. It won't kill you, though, or even make you very sick.'

'Let me hold it, so that it knows the feel of me.'

'Mind you keep it away from the baby,' said Mrs Jefferson in alarm. 'I'd sooner that you took it in another room entirely.'

As the pastor of the Oneida Full Gospel Tabernacle Church let the snake coil around his wrists, Morton said: 'What will you do, invite your congregation to come up and handle it with you as a test of faith?'

'Something like that.'

'Seriously, you want that I should come this evening and be the first in line? It sometimes helps to have somebody break the ice, as they say.'

'If you're sure that it would be no trouble for you, Mr Morton, I'd be glad to see you do so.'

'Will you be coming to the service, ma'am?' asked Morton.

'No, I reckon I'll stay at home. I suppose you want that I should take care of little Robert here?'

'If it wouldn't be an imposition.'

'No, we're becoming good friends.'

The baby still appeared drowsy and relaxed, in sharp contrast with the way that he had been in Morton's company before they arrived here. Jack Morton supposed that women just had a natural talent for soothing babies, that it was something that men were no good at.

The Oneida Full Gospel Tabernacle Church met in a somewhat plain, one almost have said severe, building two miles from the Jeffersons' home. There was no stained glass, lithographs of the

Holy Family, carved Stations of the Cross; indeed, no decoration of any description was to be found in the church. Morton took his place in a pew at the back, ready to play the part of a shill. This was something of a novelty for him; he not having acted the part since first acquiring the outfit from Abernathy.

The service was boisterous and loud, being interspersed with cries of 'Yea Lord!' and 'Preach it, brother!' from the members of the congregation. It was Jack Morton's fancy that these were among the poorer citizens of Oneida, for whom religion was a consolation against the deficiencies of their everyday life. There were raucous hymns, much clapping and cries of ecstasy. It put Morton in mind of a Negro church that he had once happened to attend.

Then came the great moment when the Reverend Jefferson quoted or, it might not inaptly be said, bellowed those verses from the Gospels that urge the faithful to fool about with rattlers and hand round cups of poison. He lifted up his voice to the Lord and then, with a mighty flourish, produced the largest and fattest rattlesnake that any of those present had ever seen. A murmur of amazement rippled round the church.

'Brothers and sisters,' said Jefferson, 'I tell you now that you belong to a generation which is blessed in the sight of the Lord. Why are you so blessed? Because this day you are seeing prophecy fulfilled. Just as our Lord said, nearly two thousand years ago, that we should be able to handle serpents with impunity, so it has now come to pass.

'This snake will by no means harm me, nor will it hurt any one of you who has the faith to come up here and hold it. Is it not written in the Book of Isaiah that the suckling child shall play on the hole of the asp and that that deadly snake shall do him no harm? Who will demonstrate his his faith by coming up here now and handling this diamondback?'

There was no rush to volunteer; Morton thought that this was just exactly what it was like when he was peddling his snake oil. It needed one or two to step forth first and then others would follow.

'I trust in the Lord!' he cried aloud. 'I reckon I'll hold that rattler and not be harmed.' He stood up and walked down the aisle to where the Reverend Jefferson was standing. He stretched out his hand and received the snake.

Just as Morton had expected, others came forward now. One by one they held his snake. Some parents even took the prophet Isaiah literally and brought their children up to stroke the rattlesnake. Morton had not expected this and hoped that no child would get bitten. The amount of venom left in the fangs after 'milking' would only give an adult a headache and fever, but could very well be sufficient to kill a child.

In the event nobody was bitten, but

Morton was glad when the service was over and his snake had been returned to the tea chest, which was hidden out of sight up in the pulpit. Morton left with the other worshippers, then doubled back so that he and the minister could carry the tea chest together back to Jefferson's house. As they walked along, Morton remarked: 'I thought that went well enough. I was worried when those children came up, though. I'm not sure that a bite from this thing would agree with a youngster.'

'Where's your faith, man? Don't you believe what I said from Isaiah?'

'I reckon had you believed it fully yourself you wouldn't have asked me if this snake of mine had been milked recently. You were careful enough of your own safety.'

The Reverend Jefferson decided to change the subject. 'You'll eat with us again this evening, I hope?' he said. 'This is the biggest and most dangerous-looking serpent I've ever had to show. I feel the least I can do is offer you our hospitality.'

'I wouldn't say no. Thank you.'

When they were back at Jefferson's house Morton was surprised to find that Robert was still sleepy and quiescent.

'It's little short of a miracle, ma'am,' he said to Mrs Jefferson. 'All the time he was with me that child was fussing and crying. A short time with you and he turns into the most amenable of creatures. I truly don't know how you do it.'

'Oh, folk often say I've a way with children. I look after babies sometimes, you see and they can be with me all day — and all night too, for the matter of that, and they're just fine.'

They ate a light meal together. Morton tried to chat amiably to the minister, but he had the distinct impression that Jefferson was still offended at the idea that he and Morton were in some way similar. It didn't much matter to Jack Morton; it was nothing to him if a man wished to maintain some pretence, even to his own self, about his nature.

When he was getting ready to leave Morton had a great shock. It happened when he picked up Robert and was about to ask Habakkuk Jefferson to give him a hand back to the livery stable with the tea chest containing his rattler.

When Morton picked up the baby his nostrils were assailed for the merest fraction of a second with a familiar, sickly smell that conjured up vivid memories of the aftermath of battle. So awful were the associations triggered by the sweet odour that, for a moment, Morton felt faint. Then he collected himself and considered from where the smell could be emanating. He sniffed delicately, then more forcefully. Strange to say, and against all reason, it was the baby himself who appeared to be the source. Morton bent down and found that he was not mistaken; the child's breath reeked of the stuff. He turned to Mrs Jefferson.

'What have you been feeding this

infant in my absence?' he asked sternly.

'Feeding him? He ain't ate a mouthful.'

'You've given him something. I know that smell well enough.'

'Oh that?' she said easily. 'I give all the little ones I have here the same thing. I get it from the drugstore. Lordy, there's no need to make such a fuss.' She went off to the kitchen and returned with a small glass bottle, which she handed to Morton. 'See now, like it says on the label, it's infant preserver.'

The label on the bottle announced:

Atkinson & Barker's
Royal
INFANTS' PRESERVATIVE
THE BEST MEDICINE
IN THE WORLD
FOR THE PREVENTION
AND CURE OF
THOSE DISORDERS
INCIDENT TO INFANTS,
NAMELY;

Convulsions, Flatulency, Affections of the Bowels,
Difficulties in Teething Etc Etc.
May be given safely, from birth onwards!

Morton removed the cork from the bottle and sniffed; almost gagging on the stench.

'Do you know what this is?' he asked fiercely. 'What you've given this baby — and others, from what you tell me? It's laudanum, ma'am. Laudanum! We used it in the army when men were badly hurt. It's tincture of opium. This child's quiet because you've drugged him.'

The Reverend Jefferson decided to step in and support his wife.

'This outrage comes oddly from you, Mr Morton,' he said. 'You make your living from selling such things, do you not?'

This was unanswerable so Morton said no more, simply gathering up Robert's clothes and diapers before bidding Mrs Jefferson a somewhat frosty goodnight. It was no simple matter to carry the baby in one arm and also help to carry the tea chest along with Jefferson. Somehow, they managed it, though, and reached the livery stable where Morton proposed to spend the night in his van. He shook hands with the Reverend Jefferson.

'It's been interesting seeing another use for my rattler, I will allow,' he said. 'Thank your wife for the food.' The two men parted on reasonably amicable terms.

5

It was still light and Morton wasn't altogether ready yet to sleep. He couldn't have stayed any longer with the Jeffersons, though, and he thought that cutting short his visit in that way was probably the smartest move. He might have said something he'd have regretted had he remained much longer in the company of that foolish woman. Fancy dosing up an innocent baby with laudanum, just to keep it quiet.

Then, because he was a man who tried his best to be honest with his own self, no matter what tricks he might be pulling on others, Jack Morton considered the question fairly. After a few minutes' thought he was forced to concede that whoever produced that damned 'infant preservative' was, as the Reverend Jefferson had said, in the same line of work as he was. This was a sobering and disagreeable notion.

While his mind was running along in this way Morton walked up and down outside the livery stable; the baby in his arms was waking up and beginning to make irritable sounds again. Probably it was time to offer him some food and drink again. Morton walked into the barn where his van was stored. His rib was still very sore, but it felt as though it was healing correctly, which was a mercy. Morton had been a little anxious that because he hadn't been able to rest then the bone might not knit together properly. It was still painful as he hoisted himself up into the back of the van with one hand while clutching the baby with the other.

After drinking some milk and smearing a little of the pap around his mouth, Robert became more cheerful, burbling and smiling at Morton.

'You're not a bad little fellow,' Morton told the child. 'Perhaps when you can speak you'll make better company for a man.' He looked into the infant's eyes and smiled, being delighted to receive an answering smile from the gurgling child. Then, from outside the van, he heard somebody say: 'I know you're in there, you son of a bitch. I can hear you talking. Howsoever many o' you there are, you best all come out with your hands held high!'

This was unexpected and Jack Morton was by no means sure how to deal with the situation. He laid the baby on the wooden boards, then picked up his pistol, which he'd left near at hand. He didn't cock it because a sharp-eared person might hear that slight metallic click and start firing on his own account first.

'Who are you and what would you have of me?' Morton said loudly.

'Never mind my name, just you come and show yourself. It's my business to set a watch upon this barn and all the other places hereabouts.'

'You a peace officer?'

'Never you mind. Just come on out.'

The voice was pitched high and had a reedy quality about it, which suggested great age to Morton. Taking a chance, he put down the pistol and went to the back of the van. A very old man with a bristling white beard was standing there, a scattergun cradled in his arms.

'Didn't I tell you to raise them hands?' he said sharply.

'Are you the night watchman?'

'What if I am?'

'Because this is my van, you damned fool. What do'you mean by pointing a gun at me?'

The old man lowered his weapon. 'I ain't a mind reader,' he said, not in the least abashed. 'Why'nt you just tell me?' Then, something struck him and he raised the gun again. 'Say, just hang on a minute there. I mind that I heard you speaking to somebody in there. Why ain't your partner come out as well?'

'Because he can't walk.'

'Can't walk? What is he, a cripple or something? There's something mighty strange about this whole set-up.'

'You want that I should fetch him out here?' asked Morton. 'I'm sure he'd be pleased to meet you.'

'Yeah, go on. But mind you move real slow. I got you covered.'

Morton turned back to the interior of his van and went over to where young Robert was sitting, chuckling to himself. He picked up the child and then went to present him to the night watchman.

'You might want to put that gun of yours entirely down,' said Morton. 'I don't want you killing me and this child both, by accident.'

When he had done as Morton suggested the old man came closer to the van and looked up at Robert.

'He's a cheerful looking little fellow,' he said. 'How come you got the charge of him? Your wife dead or something?'

'It's a long story and not one I want to go into. You going to leave us be now?'

The old man reached up his hand.

'My name's Jim Collard,' he said.

'Most everybody in these parts calls me Jim, or old Jim, so you might as well do the same.' The two men shook and Collard continued: 'I got a little cubby-hole across the way, where I brew up coffee. You want a cup?'

'That's a right welcome offer, Jim. My name's Jack and you may as well call me so. I can't be doing with any 'sir' or 'Mr Morton' or stuff like that.' As the three of them went across to the hay barn standing near to the barn where the van was being kept, it occurred to Morton that this old-timer would be the perfect individual to pump about getting to Claremont. Once they had settled down with their coffee and Jim Collard had taken young Robert on his lap and was playing with him in the pleasantest way you could imagine, Morton said: 'How far is Claremont from here? You know the town?'

'Lord, what would you be wanting to travel there for?'

''Cause this little boy's folks live

there and I promised I'd see him safe with them. How far is it?'

'In distance? Maybe forty miles. I wouldn't recommend that you attempt the journey right now though, and that's a fact.'

'How so?' asked Morton, 'What's to do?'

'You been living in cave or something?' asked Jim Collard. 'Everybody in Texas knows about the trouble hereabouts. Everybody 'cept you, I s'pose I should say. You really don't know?'

'Old man, I've had a trying few days and my store of patience ain't what you might call extensive. Would you mind telling me what the Sam Hill you're talking about? I only recently fetched up in this state.'

'That'd about account for it, I guess. It's easy enough. You know we've had all kinds of mischief from Indians — Comanche and Kiowa in the main?'

'It's not uncommon. What of it?'

'Round here it ain't just the Indians

93

we've to consider. There's all the comancheros as well. You know who they are?'

'Yes, I've had dealings with them in the past. Bandits, traders, what have you. They buy and sell stuff with the Indians. You going to tell me where this is all leading?'

'You are the most impatient young fellow I met for quite a while, you know that? The long and the short of it is that what with all the raiding by the Indians and them being helped by the comancheros, the army had to come down to put a stop to all the nonsense. They're currently quartered near Claremont; the word is that any day now they're goin' to descend on those comancheros and their friends like a duck on a June bug. Road you want, running to Claremont, that goes plumb through where the hottest part o' the action's like to be. Place called Palo Duro Canyon.'

'Is there any other way to this Claremont?'

'Not really. You'd need to make a detour of perhaps a hundred miles to get there, if you didn't use the road. Even then, you'd be going over open country, not on any road.'

'You really think things are going to get hot between here and Claremont?' asked Morton.

'No doubt at all about it. General Sheridan's arrived now and they see he's going to take personal charge of the campaign.'

Morton snorted derisively. 'Campaign! A handful of Indians and a few bandits? Much glory that will bring the army!'

Jim Collard shrugged. 'You asked how things stood and I told you,' he said. 'What you do's up to you, I guess. But I wouldn't be taking a helpless infant down that road and that's a fact.'

Later, as he was trying to settle down to sleep for the night in his van, Morton found that Robert was restless and grizzly again, as the effects of the laudanum wore off.

'Laudanum, indeed!' he muttered, as the memory came back to him. 'I never heard the like.' Then an idea struck him. Although, of course, feeding a baby opium to sedate it was a foolish and wrongheaded thing to do, would there be any harm in using his own preparation? Hadn't Reverend Jefferson's wife told him that the child was crying because he was teething? What was that, other than a pain in the gums?

From his own experience Jack Morton knew that his snake oil could genuinely alleviate the pain of aching muscles, at least to some slight degree. The camphor and red pepper combined to produce a soothing warmth that eased pains. Would they have the same effect upon the tender gums of a teething baby?

At first he hesitated because he had been a little sharp with Mrs Jefferson for the use of that 'Infant's Preservative'. Would it be any better using snake oil to soothe the child? Then he reasoned the matter through and decided that he wasn't intending actually to get the little fellow to drink the concoction, merely to smear a little on his aching gums. In the end it was the constant crying that settled the question.

There was certainly no shortage of supplies of Professor Cornelius Murgatroyd's liniment to be found and Morton reached a bottle out from one of the crates. He removed the cork and then moistened a fingertip with the liquid. Very cautiously he rubbed the fingertip gently over the baby's gums and was rewarded with a look of surprise. The crying stopped almost at once and Morton thought to himself that he had scored a bull there.

Every hour or so, Robert would rouse himself and whimper a little, then Morton would rub a little more snake oil round his gums and the baby would quieten down again. The night passed relatively peacefully in this way, with the two of them snuggled down on Morton's bedroll.

It was without a doubt a novel situation for the man, but he'd had worse and more disturbed nights than this in his life and, come the morning, he felt reasonably chipper.

'Well, young Robert,' he said to the baby when once the two of them were awake, 'I'm inclined to take a chance on this run to Claremont. In my experience, folk often make a lot of fuss and pretend matters are more serious than they actually are. I make no doubt that we'll get along famously down that road, without seeing hide nor hair of soldiers, Indians or comancheros.'

The baby stared at him solemnly, which prompted Morton to remark whimsically, 'As you raise no objection, I'll warrant you think my plan a sound one. Let's buy some provisions and then set off as soon as may be.'

The sight of a tough and capable-looking man buying boiled milk and food suitable for a weaned infant was not a common one in the stores of Oneida; Jack Morton found himself the theme of general conversation wherever he went. The men wondered what his game was and the women thought that there was something full of pathos in the idea of a man trying to care for a baby like that.

Morton wasn't in the habit of inviting direct questions about his life and doings, so nobody asked outright what was going on and how he had come by the infant but, nevertheless, he was aware that he was the centre of attention. It was a relief to be on the road again, heading north for Claremont.

It wasn't practical, neither was it agreeable to either of them, for the entire journey to proceed with the little boy perched on Morton's lap while he was driving. Robert wriggled so much and squawked so harshly that in the end Morton let him crawl around in the back of the van.

He was aware that perhaps letting a barely weaned infant roam about an enclosed space containing a large diamondback rattlesnake would not recommend itself to everybody as the ideal scheme for childcare, but there was little to be done. He ensured that the lid to the tea chest was fastened on tight and the crates of liniment covered with a tarp.

From what he'd seen of the child he was not yet at that stage of development that would enable him to clamber over the wooden slat at the back of the van and so go tumbling to destruction from the moving vehicle. After giving the baby's gums a last wipe of liniment, Morton shook the reins, crying, 'Giddyup there!'

They travelled for the whole morning without stopping. Every so often Morton would glance back into the van to assure himself that he hadn't lost his youthful passenger. The swaying motion of the van evidently had a soporific effect upon the child, because he slept for much of the way.

About midday, judging by the height of the sun in the sky, they stopped to eat. They had travelled perhaps twenty miles, which meant that with good fortune they might be in Claremont in another twenty-four hours. Obviously, they could not drive all the night long, but the going was good and there was no reason why they couldn't make another ten miles before nightfall, leaving only ten miles to be completed the following day. *So far, so good,* thought Morton. *I knew all that talk of bloodshed and war was so much hooey.*

The mealtime was a relaxed affair, with Robert crawling round and coming over to Morton for spoonfuls of the porridgy mess that appeared to satisfy all the child's dietary requirements. That and sips of milk seemed to be all that he needed.

A thing that Jack Morton had noticed time and again over the years was the way that, just when everything was going well and all your cards were falling right where you wished them to, it was right then that providence was in the habit of dealing you a few wild cards. So it proved on that particular day, when they were thirty miles or so from Oneida and Morton had persuaded himself that nothing could possibly go wrong with his plans.

The first intimation of trouble came from the merest smudge of cloud on the distant horizon. It was, like that harbinger of disaster of which Scripture tells, no bigger than a man's hand. Morton and the child had had the road entirely to themselves so far that day. It looked as though everybody else believed the rumours of war circulating and thought it safer to delay their journeys until a less hazardous season. This suited Morton well enough and he had enjoyed the solitary ride.

At first, he assumed that the little greyish cloud was dust kicked up by a rider. It pretty soon became apparent that there were more than one or two riders heading in their direction. By the time he knew that there must be at least two or three dozen men on horseback there was little Morton could do about it. His van would be shaken to pieces off the road unless he either carried on north or turned tail and tried to outrun those coming towards him.

Jack Morton had no especial prejudice against executing what, in his army days, was known as a 'strategic withdrawal', but on a purely practical level he couldn't see the nag that was drawing his van and had already put in about twenty miles that day, succeeding in outrunning men on horseback. He'd just have to take the chances as they came. Robert was asleep on the bedroll, so Morton just checked that his pistol was loose in his belt and all the cylinders primed. Then he shook the reins and carried on down the road.

When the body of riders was three miles or so from him Morton could see the white flash of feathers on their heads, along with the coppery sheen of bare skin. It was a group of Indians. By straining his eyes Morton could make out a few travois. This was promising. It might mean that this was just a bunch of wanderers, moving from one hunting ground to another. If these boys were on the warpath then surely they would not wish to burden themselves with several travois? He reined in and waited. If they wished to kill him and the child, then there was little enough that he could do about it. There were at least thirty riders coming along the road. He would just have to see what attitude they were minded to adopt.

As the men approached little Robert woke up in the back of the van and began to cry.

'You picked the right time there, boy!' said Morton. There was nothing for it but to fetch the child out and set him on his lap. He had a bottle of snake oil lying on the buckboard and he absent-mindedly popped out the cork and applied a liberal dose to the crying child's gums. The effect was magical, because Robert at once fell silent. Then, when he caught sight of the horses heading towards them, he began gurgling and pointing at them excitedly.

'They ain't acoming to entertain us, you know,' Morton told him. 'Like as not they're going to cut our throats.' Then, even though the child couldn't understand him, Morton felt a little ashamed at speaking so. He might himself be ready to die if need be, but this little fellow was a different story altogether. He stroked the boy's head and bent over to whisper softly in his ear: 'Don't be afeared. I'm telling you now, once for all, as long as I have breath in my body, I'm going to see that no harm befalls you. Even if it means giving up on my own life.' Even as he said this so lightly to the innocent baby in his arms, Jack Morton knew that he was pronouncing a solemn vow.

One problem that Morton had with Indians was that you never knew what they were thinking. The young men trotting towards him now might have been coming to invite him to a barn dance or they might equally well be fixing to scalp him. He had no idea at all. When the riders were twenty yards away, they halted. Their faces were quite expressionless, giving not the remotest hint as to their intentions. The travois came up more slowly, being dragged at a leisurely pace by the tough little ponies.

There were three travois and Morton saw that an old woman was sitting upon the packs and equipment of one of them. When the pony pulling this particular travois halted, the woman got down and stretched herself before walking in a slow and stately way to where the stand-off had developed between him and the young warriors.

Jack Morton was no ethnologist and wouldn't have cared to venture even a tentative opinion on what tribe these people belonged to. He guessed Kiowa or Comanche, because of what the old night watchman had said. From all that he was able to collect these boys were ready for action, because they were certainly armed to the teeth and, now that they had stopped, it was clear that every mother's son of them had a weapon in his hands, ranging from rifles to lances and bows. *This might be a mite tricky*, thought Morton.

The old woman, whose face was as shrivelled and wrinkled as could be, walked slowly up to the young men on horseback, then continued forward to Morton. Just at that very moment Robert began crying and there was a stirring among the Indians. Seemingly, none of them had taken note up to that point that Morton had a baby sitting on his lap.

The old woman came right up, past the horse, until she was standing only a few feet away. The little boy was still making mewling sounds and the woman looked at him, her eyes creased in what might have been the beginnings of a smile. She said something to Morton, which he could not understand. He figured that she was most likely talking Kiowa or something.

'Sorry, ma'am,' he said politely, shrugging to show what he meant, 'I can't make head nor tail o' that.'

She repeated the words, but they still made no sense at all to Morton. Then the woman stretched out her arms and the gesture was plain. She was asking him to hand her the baby. He hesitated, but then took a chance. She was, after all, a woman and her face was kindly and wise.

'I don't mind you dandling the little fellow for a minute or two,' he said, 'if that's what you're asking for.'

Very slowly, making quite certain that he did not do anything that could be open to misinterpretation, Morton climbed down from the buckboard, holding Robert in the crook of his left arm. When he was standing on the ground, he walked over to the old woman.

'Mind,' he said, 'I trust you to hand him back again afterwards.' Her face gave nothing away and he had no idea at all if she had understood what he said. Morton held out the infant to her and she at once reached out her arms to receive him.

Almost as soon as young Robert was being held by the old Indian woman he ceased crying and stared curiously at her face. She smiled toothlessly at him and the baby chuckled.

'Well,' said Morton, 'I reckon you've made a friend there all right.' He did not know how things were going to pan out, but he was convinced that this woman meant no harm to the baby he was charged to take care of.

Still not sure if she understood him or not, Morton spoke again.

'I'll be having that child back again now, ma'am, if it's all the same to you. I promised to deliver him to his kin and I've still some way to go.' The old woman looked at him and smiled once more. Then she turned her back on him and headed back to the party of braves waiting a few yards away. Without any doubt she proposed to hang on to the baby for herself.

6

When Morton realized what was happening: that somebody was making off with the child he'd sworn to protect, he took a pace or two after the Indian woman, not even thinking what he was doing. There was the click of a gun being cocked and two of the warriors took arrows from quivers and fitted them to their bows. The old woman said something, though, and nothing happened.

The young men continued to stare menacingly at Morton, however, and he understood very well that if he attempted to regain the child by main force he was apt to be shot down on the spot. There was nothing at all to be done. He stood in impotent fury as the Indians trotted past him; veering off the road to bypass his van.

As the travois carrying the old

woman and the baby for whom he was responsible passed him Morton was tempted to rush forward and snatch Robert back. Perhaps something of what was going through his mind was visible on his face, because some of the young warriors watched him closely and he was certain that he would have been shot down the second he made a move.

Then they had all passed him by and Morton could only stare after the party as they disappeared down the road. He kicked a stone savagely, altogether at a loss to know what to do next. There wasn't, as far as he could see, anything to be done. He could hardly ride against thirty well-armed braves. He might as well just accept that Robert was gone and that was the end of it.

He didn't for a moment suppose that the child would come to any harm in the care of the old woman. She had looked too kind and wise for Morton to imagine that she would be hurting the little boy. Most likely, she loved children and had a hankering to have one for her own again. He had heard of such cases, where grandmothers had adopted little children and raised them as their own. Most likely, she would care for the baby better than Morton himself was able to do.

Slowly and with great reluctance Jack Morton got back up on to the driving seat and made ready to leave. Then he recollected the oath he had sworn earlier that day. He wasn't a one for churchgoing, but that had been a solemn promise made to he knew not whom. He would be acting wrongly were he do abandon that child and simply forget his vow.

Morton shook the reins. 'Giddyup!' he said loudly. Once the beast was moving Morton turned the van round in a wide circle and set off after the Indians.

The plain stretched as far as the eye could see; it was flat and almost entirely featureless, other than for a line of red sandstone cliffs that lay to the left of the road. The riders whom he had encountered were still in sight and they wouldn't, he calculated, be able to travel much faster than his van. Those three travois would ensure that they moved at a steady and not overly fast pace.

It wouldn't do at all for the men he was pursuing to know what he was about. Morton had a notion that if those boys thought that he was going to cause them any mischief they would send back a few men to make an end of him. He didn't rightly know why they hadn't killed him anyway, but he would be ill-advised to press his luck. This would take some little consideration. It wouldn't help that child if Morton just charged in and got himself killed for his pains. He reined in the horse and sat for a good quarter of an hour, reasoning things out.

One thing was definite: he wouldn't lose track of those men who had carried off Robert. Even when they were too far off for him to see them directly, the dust they kicked up would betray their whereabouts. As long as the light held Morton would be able to see where the riders were heading. Next off was to think on where they were heading. If those men and the old woman were on their way to a large village or other settled land belonging to their tribe, then the whole enterprise was hopeless. He could hardly ride this van of his through Indian country, stopping off just long enough to snatch a baby from some old female relative of theirs.

He didn't think, though, that that was what they were doing. The presence of three travois hinted that this group was either wandering, or seeking refuge somewhere. Maybe they'd been displaced by this army activity of which he'd been told. If that was the case and they were refugees, then it could be that they were the only men he'd have to contend with. Even so, he would be ill-advised to ride up against them openly, but it might mean that he could raid their camp by night.

Morton continued sitting there, watching and waiting until the Indians were quite out of view and the only indication of their presence was the grey smudge of dust hanging above them. Then he set off in pursuit.

During the War Between the States Jack Morton had been part of a group of saboteurs who had struck deep behind the Union lines. They had operated in civilian clothes, which mean that they were all liable to be hanged as spies if they were identified, but he'd never heard of any of his unit being caught. The Union forces called Morton and his comrades 'The Ghosts', due to their positively uncanny ability to slip in and out of occupied territory, inflicting maximum damage for little or no losses on their side. Posters went up describing them as bandits and murderers and offering thousands of dollars in gold for their capture, dead or alive. He had abandoned all that foolishness during the Reconstruction and had even taken the Ironclad Oath. That did not mean that he could not, in a good cause, return to those ways for just one single night.

Morton made his way along at a leisurely pace, making sure that he allowed the Indians ahead of him to be so far in advance that they would not find it convenient to dispatch a few men to investigate who else might be travelling along this road. He ran over in his mind what resources he had for the little expedition that he planned. There wasn't a great deal, to be sure.

For his rifle and pistol, Morton had a small copper flask of powder: a 'Stand of Flags' flask, which he had had since before the war. There was also a drum of camphor oil, which he used in the manufacture of his 'liniment'. That really was about it, apart from various items such as a coil of rope and so on. He'd just have to make the best of things.

Morton knew, from coming that way earlier, that the road between Oneida and Claremont ran straight as an arrow, yet the cloud in the far distance now looked to Morton to be veering to the left somewhat. He watched, intrigued. After another quarter-hour he was convinced that the Indians must have left the road and be striking out towards the cliffs. He might be wrong in his reading of the situation; it might very well be that there was a vast encampment of Kiowas or Comanches in that direction, with hundreds of comancheros milling around into the bargain; but Morton didn't think so.

He had a hunch that this little group of Indians was, for reasons at which he could only guess, on the move alone. That being so, if they were now fixing to hole up for the night in the hills that probably lay behind those red cliffs, then that would be as good a chance as he was likely to get to retrieve that child.

It was time to start moving. These days Jack Morton was not an aggressive or vindictive man, but he was most decidedly vexed with the people who had taken the baby in such a casual way. He would fetch Robert back or die in the attempt, and at the same time make damned sure that those boys knew that it would have been better to leave him be. *They've started this business*, thought Morton, *let's hope that they're ready to bide the consequences of it.*

Watching the plume of dust as it moved along ahead of him, Morton could see now that it was almost at the foot of the cliffs. Unless he missed his guess, there was some trail or path leading through the rocks there, for which the Indians were heading. It would be evening soon and they were most likely heading to some spot that they knew, where they could rest for the night.

All right then; let them do that very thing. But, unless he'd grown old and silly in those years since the war ended, Jack Morton was the man to see to it that they didn't rest easy the whole night long. He'd have that child back again before dawn.

The cloud of dust that he had been observing and by which Morton was able to see where the Indians were heading, vanished as abruptly as if it were a lamp that had suddenly been extinguished. One moment it was there and then the next it had dissipated in the glow of the early evening sun. That was no great mystery; the riders had moved from the dusty surface of the plain on to the bare rock of the sandstone formations that lay to the left of the road.

It was safe to speed up a little now, since the men he was trailing would presumably be in the canyons and gullies of the rocky hills and, before long, out of sight of the road. They would no longer be in a position to see the little bit of dust that he was himself kicking up.

Morton didn't take his eyes from the place in the cliffs where he had last seen the dust cloud. He wanted to be certain-sure of finding the same route up into the hills that the Indians had used. The cliffs were maybe a mile off from the road he was on and he was a little dubious of the ability of his van to travel over the rock-strewn land that lined the road.

When he had drawn close to where he thought the Indians had vanished into the cliffs he was pleased to note a crevice or gap in the sheer rock face. *That's a path*, he thought, or *I'm a Dutchman*.

Rather than rattle across the rough and uneven terrain, so risking a broken axle, Morton got down from the buckboard and led the horse along. That way, down closer to the ground, he could see any especially large rocks and steer round them. His horse was just about at the limit and it would be good to unharness her and allow her to eat and drink a little. They were running low on feed and the water keg was also perilously low, but Morton figured that he could perhaps go without water more easily than the horse. After all, if she gave up the ghost, then he would be in a disastrous state.

Having reached the foot of the cliffs Morton hobbled the horse and turned her loose. Then he shared the remaining water, settled down and waited for nightfall. There would be little point in setting off up that rocky trail before it was completely dark. He didn't want to tip his hand before he was ready to lay down.

As evening fell and the twilight turned slowly to night the materials he would need for his little adventure were removed, one by one, from the back of the van. There was a metal can, containing perhaps a gallon of camphor oil, a coil of rope and then his rifle. After these were arranged neatly on the ground, he climbed in one final time and brought out the powder flask. He weighed this carefully in his hand and gauged there to be perhaps three ounces of powder in it.

There were too many imponderables

in the operation for Morton's liking, but there was precious little that could be done about that. He would have to play the hand he'd been dealt, not the one he would have chosen had he been able to fix the deck beforehand.

When it was quite dark he slung the rope over his shoulder, tucked the flask of powder into his pants pocket, picked up the can of camphor oil in one hand and his rifle with the other and set off up the path leading through the cliffs. The night was a little chilly, although not actually cold, and Morton hoped devoutly that the men he was hunting for had seen fit to light a fire that evening; if only to cook their evening meal on. Otherwise his scheme was apt to miscarry at once. When he reached the top of the slope, though, his sensitive nostril caught the acrid tang of wood smoke. There was a fire going not far from where he stood.

What little experience he had of Indians led Morton to think that they would most likely go to sleep as soon as it got dark, then rise at first light. Would they put a sentry on duty? He would have to keep a wary eye out for that.

The path snaked through the cliffs and then came out on to a little plateau. It was a new moon, which gave him the cover of darkness. Below, in a natural rocky amphitheatre nestling in the hills, he could see the ruddy glow of a campfire. Nearer at hand he could just make out the silhouette of a man who was seated on a boulder, his head resting on his chest, giving the impression of a fellow enjoying a refreshing nap.

Very carefully, Morton set down the can of camphor oil and then reversed the rifle, so that he could swing the butt at a handy target. Then he drove the rifle with his full strength against the sleeping man's head, sending him flying backwards off the rock upon which he had been perched. Had this been a genuine military operation Morton would have made sure to kill the fellow before proceeding further, but he was reluctant to shed blood without good cause and, after the blow he'd been dealt, Morton could not imagine that man being able to get up and fight for several hours yet. He picked up the can of camphor oil and made his way gingerly down the slope to where the fire glowed faintly.

When he was almost at the bottom of the slope Morton paused again and stood perfectly still, listening. He had thought that the travois he saw might have been carrying a couple of tepees, but in the embers of the campfire, he could see that in fact the travellers were sleeping in wickiups, built from branches and twigs woven together. He doubted they could have thrown these up in the time available, so Morton figured that this must be a regular stopping-over site for members of the tribe, whoever they were.

There was no sign of anybody being awake so Morton set to work. In a sheath on his belt he carried a razor-sharp knife and this he drew.

There were thirty or so horses, all contained in a little corral made of thorny branches lashed together with rawhide thongs. That would not take long to dismantle. He set to, slashing the leather strips apart and carefully teasing out branches, so that the beasts were able to go free when they chose. They might need a little encouragement, but he was sure that he would be able to supply that.

Very carefully, Morton moved round the encampment, listening at every hut. He found the one that he was seeking last of all. Within, he could hear the unmistakable snuffling and little cries of a fretful baby. The odds, he supposed, were stacked very much against there being two young infants around here.

Little though he knew about the ways of Indians, it seemed reasonable to assume that the only woman, specially an exceedingly old one, in a party of men would have a wickiup all to herself and that she would have the baby with her. Morton, unwound a length of rope and cut it from the coil. Then he set down the can of oil by the opening that served as a door for the crude hut, ducked his head and entered.

He was in no mood to fool around, so, much as it went against his general principles to manhandle a woman, he started by ensuring that the old woman would not interfere, nor raise the alarm. He could just about see in the gloom, where a body was lying, and from the sounds that the came from the other side of the wikiup he was able to hear that Robert was not next to the woman.

The sooner this business was concluded the better. Morton brushed his hands over the sleeping body to establish which end had feet, then grabbed hold of the head at the opposite end of the body, clamping a hand over the mouth to stifle any cries. Then he forced the length of rope in the old woman's mouth and tied it securely at the back of her head, effectually gagging her. Working swiftly, he used the larger coil to tie her hands behind her back and then secure them to her feet. He was firm, but not rough. When this was done he went over to where the baby lay and scooped him up in his arms.

So far, so good. Robert hadn't woken, for which Morton was profoundly grateful. As he left the hut he reached into his pocket and extracted the powder flask. Holding this awkwardly in the same hand with which he was supporting the baby, he picked up the can of camphor oil and unscrewed the top. There was a stack of broken branches and twigs near the dying campfire. Morton threw some oil on to the embers, hoping that the fire would rekindle more vigorously.

When flames began to flicker he carefully placed the can of oil on the fire and then dropped the copper flask of powder next to it. Then he sprinted up towards the path that led back to his horse and van. He was almost at the point where he had lamped the sentry when there came the sharp crack of an explosion, followed almost instantly by a blinding white flash that lit up the whole area like a lightning bolt. Just as Morton had planned, the powder flask had gone off like a grenade, shattering the tin of boiling camphor oil and allowing the fire to ignite it at once.

Also as he had hoped and expected, the horses were driven mad by the sudden exploding gunpowder and brilliant white light of the blazing camphor oil. They stampeded out of the flimsy corral, headed away from Morton and thundered through a gap in the depression. *I bet they take a bit of catching*, he thought. Then it was time to make his way make down the path to the van. Just before he began threading his way down, Jack Morton turned towards the little encampment and said quietly: 'Well, I reckon that if we meet again, you boys will know to give me a wide berth and not go troubling me or aught.'

Since the Indians would not know where the attackers were coming from, nor how many there were, Morton guessed that he would be safe from pursuit for quite some time, particularly since they would be fully occupied for the rest of the night in trying to catch their horses. His main fear, once he had harnessed up again and was leading the horse and van back to the road, was that in the darkness he would miss some rock and damage his only means of escape from the area. But God sometimes smiles on villains and fools, as well as the righteous, and he made the road with no mishap.

It had been one of those nights when sleep was going to be quite out of the question, so Morton resigned himself to riding the moon out of the sky. By dawn he believed that he had put five miles between himself and any pursuit by vengeful Indians. He really had no desire to be caught out here in the wilderness by a body of swift warriors on horseback and he kept glancing back anxiously to check that there was no sign of that happening. The sun had only been above the horizon for perhaps a quarter-hour when Morton knew that his hopes were vain and that a number of galloping horses were heading after him.

The dusty cloud raised by the riders was spreading along the road, so fast were the horsemen riding, and unless he'd lost his skills as a scout Jack Morton believed that they would be upon him in no more than fifteen minutes. Whoever they were, and he could have a pretty good guess at the identity of those racing towards him so frantically, they were in the devil of a hurry.

There was no point even trying to outrun them. His horse was tired and in sore need of a proper rest. All that Morton could do was try and pick them off before they reached him. Then he recalled, with a sinking heart, that he had used the only powder he possessed in that reckless gamble at the Indian camp. His rifle was charged for one shot and he had another five shots in the pistol at his belt. His chances suddenly did not look too brilliant.

Never having been one for giving up without a fight, Morton did not mean to begin now. He reined in the horse and then peered back into the van. Robert was still asleep, which was a mercy. Morton took the rifle, jumped down and positioned himself behind one of the wheels. Then, realizing that he had just done something incredibly foolish, he stood up again and went back to secure the brakes. He returned to his position, knelt down and trained the rifle on the cloud of dust that indicated he might have only ten minutes of life remaining to him. He cocked his piece and waited.

As the riders came closer he was able to see that they were not, after all, Indians. All the same, nobody else seemed to be using this road, so the sight of these three men racing along made Morton a little curious. He remained where he was and continued to keep his rifle pointing in their general direction. Who knew? They could be road agents or the Lord knew what else. He wasn't about to take any chances, not now that he had that baby back in his care.

7

'Who are you?' cried one of the men as they reined in a little way off from the van. 'Will you hold the road against us?'

'I ain't holding the road,' called back Morton. 'The three of you can go round me, if you're minded.'

'Morton?' shouted back the man, 'Jack Morton! What in the hell are you doing out here?'

'Is that you, Robarts? You and your friends mean no harm?'

'Not a bit of it. Come out and talk, man. What ails you, why are you hiding behind that van?'

Morton stood up and lowered his rifle. He walked over to where Emile Robarts waited along with two other men who looked as though they too could be Creoles or perhaps Mexican. Morton reached up his hand and shook with the three of them.

'As I live and breathe,' Robarts said, 'what in the name of all that's wonderful brings you out here, Morton?'

At that moment Robert began to cry lustily. 'Wait up,' Morton said, 'I have to feed the child.' He climbed aboard the van, picked up the baby and the jar of food, then went back to talk to the riders, who were watching him and his actions with increasing amazement.

'You taken up as a nursemaid? What's with the baby?' Robarts asked.

'It's a long story,' replied Morton as he spooned the pap awkwardly into the infant's mouth, while endeavouring to avoid dropping the jar, the spoon or the baby. 'You didn't see any Indians heading along the same way that you came, did you?'

'They don't mostly use the road right now,' replied Robarts. 'Word is that the army are going to be using this route soon. You remember that bastard

Sheridan? General Sheridan as he is now? He'll be here directly to winkle out all the Kiowas and Comanches to take 'em off to some reservation. But why? You have trouble?'

Briefly, Morton told the men of his little escapade the night before. The three of them stared at him in horror.

'You've not changed since the surrender, Morton,' Robarts observed. 'You still know how to get yourself into a heap of trouble. You best come along with us.'

Robarts's two companions looked uneasy and one of them said something in a low voice.

'Morton hates the Yankees as much as we do,' Robarts told them. 'He and me fought side by side, behind the lines. He won't betray us.'

'I thank you kindly for the offer,' said Morton, 'but the fact of the matter is, I have to get this child to Claremont. It's been good visiting with you Robarts, and I'd love to talk over old times, but my business is pressing.'

'You won't make it to Claremont,' said Robarts briefly. 'For one thing, the army are going to be coming up that road and they'll most likely be fighting along the way. More to the point, that old woman you tied up and assaulted sounds to be mighty like the old chief's wife, mother of the present chief of the Kiowa, Mamay Day Te. That's the boy we call Lone Wolf in English.

'I heard that he'd sent his mother refugeeing down towards Oneida with a nice bodyguard. When word reaches Lone Wolf of what you did, your life won't be worth shit. You want to save your life and that of the baby there, you best accompany us.'

Robarts was, according to Morton's recollections, a man of few words. Such a long speech as this indicated that he felt strongly about the subject. If a man like Emile Robarts told you your life was in danger, then it was wise to sit up and take note. Morton shrugged.

'It doesn't seem like I have a deal of choice in the matter,' he said.

After they'd been on their way for a while, with Robarts riding alongside the van, Morton said: 'I thought this was the way to Claremont? Didn't you say that General Sheridan was apt to come charging along here soon?'

'We're not going the whole length of the road. We turn off soon and make for the canyon.'

'What canyon might that be?'

'Place called Palo Duro. Ever heard of it?'

'Not until a day or two back, I hadn't. Isn't that where the Indians and the comancheros are supposed to be holed up?'

'That's it, in a nutshell.'

'What makes you so sure that those comancheros'll give me a warm welcome? You in with them?'

'You might say so,' said Robarts, laughing. 'I suppose you'd have to know sooner or later. I lead a band of them. Biggest bunch hereabouts.'

'You, Robarts? That makes strange listening.'

'Don't see why. I'm still fighting the Yankees, same as during the war. Is that any stranger than selling snake oil?'

Morton laughed at that, a long rich chuckle.

'That shot was in the gold! You're right, we've all of us had to find other ways of making a living since the war. Listen, do you really think that this Lone Wolf will be vexed with me for hogtying his ma?'

'Man, are you quite crazy? He'll hunt you down to the ends of the earth to kill you slowly. He sets great store by his mother, I'm telling you.'

'She shouldn't have taken little Robert here. It was her as started the business.'

'That's nothing to the purpose. We're going to be near the Comanches. They're like to find the story amusing, should they hear of it. Not that I recommend you shoot your mouth off about it.'

At about midday they reached a pool fed by some spring that had its origins among the hills and cliffs to their right. The horses were allowed to drink their fill while the four men walked about and stretched their limbs.

Robarts introduced his partners, who looked to Jack Morton like typical *vaqueros*, as Rod and Casso. Presumably these were abbreviations of some kind, Morton guessed that Rod was probably short for 'Rodriguez', but in any event, those were the names to which they answered.

They appeared to be reasonable enough fellows, and if Robarts trusted them Morton was inclined to go along with his old comrade. Emile Robarts had always been a sound judge of character.

From what he could make out, Palo Duro Canyon and the villages there for which they were heading were about another four hours away. It was good of the riders to travel along at the slow pace of his van. To Morton's surprise, none of the other three men showed any real interest in how he had come to be responsible for a baby. That was the good thing about associating with those on the wrong side of the law; it was considered ill mannered to take too much notice of another fellow's affairs, let alone ask a heap of questions.

Morton returned the compliment and didn't ask where Robarts and the others had been or what they were up to in the canyons. He hazarded a private guess that it was perhaps something in the gunrunning line, but it wasn't really any of his business.

Before they set off again, Morton contrived to speak privately to Emile Robarts.

'Listen man,' he said, 'you see how I'm placed, having charge of this infant and all?'

'It's nothing to me,' said Robarts with a laugh. 'You say you're answer-able for the child, that's good enough for me.'

'Yeah, I knew you'd adopt that line and I'm thankful for it. What I want to know though is this. Are you quite sure that going along with you boys into this canyon of yours, Palo Duro as you call it, you perfectly sure that that's safer for this infant than if I were just to make a run for Claremont down this road?'

Robarts, whose manner was now, as it had always been during the war, casual and amused, placed his hand on Morton's shoulder.

'Old friend,' he said, 'I tell you now that if you go down that route there ahead of us, you and that child won't make it to your destination. The land there is alive with scouts, Kiowas and Comanches both. They'd kill you as a spy. I won't even talk of your attacking Lone Wolf's mother. That alone would be the death of you in these parts, even if there wasn't a war brewing.'

'Well then, all I can tell you is that I'm mighty glad of your help.'

Palo Duro Canyon was a vast network of smaller canyons, little valleys, streams, pools and grazing lands. You would never guess when entering the place from the road that there was such a rich and varied landscape hidden away behind the forbidding cliffs. This had been the stronghold of the Comanche and Kiowa for some years; since Texas had become an American possession, in fact.

The comancheros, most of whom were Mexican in origin, had bases here as well. They had a strong business interest in not seeing the Indians herded on to reservations. From time out of mind, the comancheros had exchanged powder and guns for ponies and hides, coffee, tobacco and alcohol for slaves and other, even less salubrious trading activities. Without the Indians, the comancheros would most likely end up being forced by economic necessity into hiring themselves out as vaqueros.

Palo Duro looked to Morton like some vision of paradise. There were herds of ponies grazing peacefully, children playing freely around the villages scattered throughout the network of valleys, and plenty of fresh water to sustain a pretty large population.

'How come you and your friends can't just live peaceably here?' he said to Robarts.

'Tell you the truth, Morton, I wouldn't mind at all. But we need flour and coffee, stuff like that. We have to trade with the rest of the state in order to get those things. There's no real agricultural land here, it's just pasture. We couldn't grow wheat, barley or anything of that kind here.'

'It sure looks nice, I must say.'

Like many people, Morton had always thought of the comancheros as being next door to bandits; it was a pleasant surprise to see that they had a settled and law-abiding aspect to them, just like other folks.

The comancheros lived a little apart from their allies and trading partners, in a little collection of wickiups in a canyon of their own. Robarts's group were not the only comancheros based in Palo Duro, and Morton gathered that some were rougher than others.

'You best keep out of sight for a while,' said Robarts, "til I've had a chance to ask about and find out how things stand. I don't think word will yet have reached anybody here about Lone Wolf's mother, but you never can tell with Indians. Sometimes, they seem to have an almost supernatural ability to hear news before any human agency could be involved.

'I'll see if any of the Kiowas hereabouts know about this. You can keep your van here with us, but I'd appreciate it if you could somehow disguise it a little, so it's not as noticeable. Maybe put brushwood over it or something. There's no point in meeting trouble halfway, leastways not until we have to.'

After Robarts and the others had gone off Morton set to and began disguising his van. It seemed the least that he could do, when those fellows had been decent enough to rescue him in that way. He surely would not like to put them in hazard as a reward for their kind actions. He moved the van closer to the wall of boulders and rocks, unharnessed the horse and then began gathering material to cover at least that absurd painted advertisement on the side of his vehicle.

As he worked, picking up lengths of brushwood and propping them against the side of the wooden contraption that had been his home for almost two years, Morton was filled suddenly with a sense of loathing for this way of earning a living. Even those like Emile Robarts and his partners, who lived on the edge of the law, could still find companionship with other like-minded men and feel some satisfaction in what he was doing.

Was it his imagination, or had Robarts looked surprised, even a little disgusted, when he saw that his former comrade was peddling snake oil for a living?

Morton was not in general given to introspection, so after he had made a good effort at concealing the identity of his van he decided to take Robert for a walk about the place. The meagre supply of diapers were all soiled and wet and he needed to find a river or pool in which to wash them.

Although the comancheros kept themselves a little apart from the Indian villages, there was no strict separation between them and their customers. There were Indians, chiefly Comanches, hanging round the camp and the comancheros themselves went often to the Comanche and Kiowa villages on various business.

So it was that, almost as soon as he had picked up the baby and set out for a stroll, Morton found that he somehow picked up a straggling band of children who followed him, vastly entertained at the sight of a grown man cradling an infant in his arms.

'You children cut along now,' growled Morton. 'You never see a baby before?'

Despite the gruffness of his mannner

the children, mainly girls, did not run away but instead began giggling and imitating the way that he was holding the baby close to his body. His escort of young children were still with Morton when he came upon a group of women washing various articles in a stream.

The women watched the approach of this strange figure: a tough, capable-looking young man carrying a baby. It was a novelty in their lives; not one of their own men would have consented to appear in public in such a character. Nursing a baby like that would have been see as a sign of rank effeminacy in any Comanche warrior. The white man, though, seemed oblivious to the stigma, merely nodding politely and saying a few brief words that they interpreted to be a friendly greeting of some sort.

He set Robert down near by and then proceeded to rinse out the diapers in the running water. The Indian women watched, lost for words. It was apparent that the sight of a man caring for a baby and washing out his clothes was not a common one around those parts.

Being the object of such attention was not really something that Morton relished. He was about to turn and walk in another direction entirely, when the focus of attention shifted abruptly away from him.

The stream from which water was fetched for the Comanche village was fed by mountain springs. It emptied into a large pool, perhaps fifty yards across, which formed a natural-rock cistern. It was here that horses were led to water, to avoid contaminating the stream.

Playing on the edge of this pool was a popular pastime for the children, who made little boats of wood, skimmed stones across its surface and told each other stories of the monster who lurked within its watery depths. The danger of the water margin was that there were no gently sloping shallows leading to the deep water. The rock fell sharply away within inches of the edge of the pool and the central portion was, at least according to legend, bottomless. If not strictly speaking bottomless, the greater part of the pool was certainly deeper than the five or six feet that would have enabled a person to wade across to the other side of the little lake.

On that particular day one of the children playing by the water's edge, a little girl aged perhaps three or four, had somehow tumbled into the water. Her frantic struggling had had the effect of carrying her away from the rocky bank and now she was floundering about twenty feet out of reach of those standing on the margin of the pool.

The child's mother, hearing the commotion of the panicking children, had rushed to the scene and was now keening and wailing in a high, unearthly lament, as though her daughter were already dead.

Along with the women who had been washing at the stream, Morton ran to the pool. He sized up the situation in a moment and realized at once that, for whatever reason, the woman screaming and tearing her hair out in distress, had no intention of jumping into the water and actually helping the drowning child.

The other women had caught up with him and were also beginning to wail and bemoan the tragedy that had befallen the helpless little girl. Yet still, not a one of them showed any sign of getting ready to rescue the child, who was now dipping below the surface.

Morton thrust Robert into the arms of one of the women and then kicked off his boots. He placed his pistol in one of the boots and then, without further ado, dived into the icy clear water of the pool.

The child had disappeared now below its placid surface and Morton knew that unless he was exceedingly swift she would sink out of reach of his help. He took a gulp of air and then went under himself. At first, he could see nothing, but then he glimpsed a shadowy disturbance ahead of him.

Morton surfaced for air and then went down again; this time seeing the child at once. She was thrashing about less now and a fear gripped his heart that unless he got her up into the air soon, she would be dead. His own lungs were bursting, but there was not a second to lose. With one last effort he lunged forward, grabbed the now limp figure and kicked his way up again into the sunlight.

The child he was grasping was as lifeless and floppy as a rag doll, but there was no time to think of that now. The only thing to be done was to get her ashore. Swimming in waterlogged clothes is a tricky enough undertaking at the best of times, but being additionally burdened with a helpless child made the whole business of reaching dry land even more arduous. When at last he made it ashore, Morton succeeded in hauling the little girl from the water, before getting out himself. The child showed not the slightest sign of life and he began to think that his efforts had all been in vain.

The women, who had fallen silent when they saw Morton hurl himself into the water, now set up another concerted wail bemoaning the death of the girl. None of them checked to see what, if anything, could be done to revive her.

Morton grabbed the lifeless body roughly and turned it over so that the face was downwards. Then he pounded hard on the tiny back and began moving the arms up and down. The women watched him as though he had taken leave of his senses. Then, to Morton's astonishment as much as theirs, the frail figure gave a convulsive jerk and gouts of water erupted from her mouth. She coughed and shuddered and then cried aloud.

She was not dead after all.

8

After he had retrieved his baby, all that Morton wished to do was go back to the van and change into dry clothes. This he was by no means permitted to do. The women shepherded him towards the village, keeping up an unintelligible commentary the whole while.

For his part, Morton made remarks such as, 'It was nothing at all!' and 'Please don't mention it.' In this way the little group arrived at the Comanche village and soon a large audience gathered, to which they related the recent and amazing events.

Morton later heard that he had been credited with raising the child from the dead and that this, together with the fact that he had first been seen carrying a baby, had raised him in the eyes of many to the position of part medicine man and part heroic warrior.

When they got to the centre of the village the woman whose child he had rescued called aloud to those present. Morton figured that she was saying something along the lines of, 'Where's that husband of mine? He has to hear this!' That he was right in his guess was confirmed when a tall, stately looking man came walking unhurriedly towards them.

The child's mother babbled a lot to this man when he arrived and he listened impassively. When she came to a halt, he looked over to where Morton was standing. Then he walked slowly over to Morton and placed his arms around his shoulders. Having done this, he raised his voice and gave a brief speech, of which Jack Morton understood not a single word.

Although he could not make out what the Indian was saying, Morton was nevertheless sensible of being praised and applauded for his actions in saving the life of the child. He shrugged when the man had finished speaking.

'It's nothing to mention,' he said. 'I just happened to have been there and I'm glad I could be of service.'

The Indian stared intently into Morton's face and then, evidently satisfied with what he saw there, he struck his own chest and rattled out a string of incomprehensible syllables, which were clearly his name. Feeling that something was expected of him in return, Morton touched his breast lightly and said: 'Morton. Glad to know you, sir.'

The Indian said, 'Morton.'

'That's my name. If it's all the same with you, I'll be getting along now to change out of these wet things.'

The man said again, 'Morton' and then, without any more ado, turned and walked off.

Morton felt a little more human once he'd put on dry clothes and tended to the baby. After Robert fell asleep Morton simply sat there, leaning against the van and thinking. The chief burden of his ruminations was that he'd more or less had enough of this racket, which was to say selling snake oil. He had something like $600 saved up, which would be enough to set him up somewhere for a while. This game had been well enough to begin with and there was no denying it paid well enough, but lately he'd begun to find a strange distaste for the trade creeping over him.

A thought came to him. An hour later, when Robarts appeared, he stood up and went over to him with the intention of broaching the subject. Before he was able to open a conversation though, Robarts spoke.

'You're the one, Morton,' he said. 'I been hearing about your exploits.'

'How's that?'

'Rescuing Stormcloud's daughter from a watery grave. Everybody's talking about Morton in that village, I tell you.'

'That's a piece of foolishness. They'd do better to learn how to swim rather than trust on some foolhardy stranger being on the scene. But listen, Robarts, I got something to ask you.'

'Go on then. Out with it.'

'It's easy enough. You looking for any new men to join your crew here?'

'You, Morton? You want to ride with us?'

'I'll lay down, so you can see how the case stands. I've had my fill of rooking hicks of their nickels and dimes for the stuff I boil up in back of my van. I've a mind to ride free again for a while.'

Emile Robart's face split into a wide grin. 'It'll be like the old days again, you and me harrying the Union forces. Of course you're welcome to join us. I was hoping you'd ask.' He stretched out his hand and Morton took it in his own firm clasp. 'Only one thing, though. What are you fixing to do with that child?'

'I'm going to run down to Claremont, hand him over to his kin, sell my van and stock and then come straight back. That all right with you?'

'Sure it is.'

Next morning there was news that surprised both Morton and Robarts. A messenger from the Comanche village brought word that Stormcloud would consider it a great honour if Morton would attend a feast that evening. The man who brought the message spoke passable English and Morton thanked him, saying that he would be there at dusk. After the messenger had departed Morton spoke to Robarts.

'This is a damned nuisance,' he said. 'I suppose it would be noticed if I didn't attend?'

'You mustn't even think of it. Stormcloud is one of my staunchest allies. Don't you start putting him out of countenance by snubbing him. You'll be there all right.'

Jack Morton had a positive horror of anything that smacked of formality. The idea of being guest of honour at some banquet was not an enticing one. He guessed that it would not differ substantially from such an event laid on by white people. There was apt to be speeches, toasts and all the rest of the nonsense. And all for the sake of his having jumped in the water and dragged out some child.

Still, there it was. Robarts was pleased about the whole episode because he clearly wished to be in with this Stormcloud, so Morton would be advancing his old friend's interests by attending. For all that, it was still a damned nuisance.

Throughout the day Morton watched Robarts's band of men coming and going, moving boxes about, talking together in low, urgent voices and checking and loading their weapons. Most of the men were Mexican or swarthy enough to be half Mexican and half white. They were friendly enough to Morton, a couple even condescending to chuck baby Robert under the chin. Morton didn't know whether or not Robarts had told them yet that he might be joining them soon. The day wore on in this fashion until the sun began sinking towards the horizon in the west.

'What should I wear for this blamed meal?' Morton asked his old comrade.

Emile Robarts laughed.

'What, you think you might need to have a stovepipe hat and a tailcoat?' he said. 'Relax, it's nothing so formal. What you have on now will do very well.'

'That's a mercy. I never feel comfortable when I'm decked out in respectable clothes. Makes me feel like a tailor's dummy. I was working the river-boats before I took up at this present game and I had to look the part there. Then after that, I've been posing as a professor and you need to dress up a mite for that, too. It'll be a relief not to have to worry about my personal appearance when I join you boys.'

'Yes,' said Robarts, 'we're not great ones for fancy outfits here.'

'Will you and the others be coming, too?'

'We ain't invited. Stormcloud seems to want you there, but not us. I'll tell you straight, that if you throw in your hand with us, this could work to our advantage. Stormcloud's a good friend of ours, but he can be the devil to treat with. If he takes to you, that could be handy.'

'Let's see how it goes, then.'

When Morton arrived at the Comanche village the children he had seen the previous day ran up and greeted him. He was carrying Robert with him, for he hardly felt able to ask a band of rough comancheros to act as nursemaids for him. The children were still endlessly entertained by the sight of a man holding a baby. The girls came up and touched Robert's head, while the boys just stared; nothing in their short lives having prepared them for such a spectacle.

When their mothers heard the commotion that signalled Morton's approach they came and shooed the children away. Word must have spread that here was a man who although behaving in some ways like a woman, being apparently attached to a small child, was also a brave man who had not hesitated to risk his own life for somebody else. As a consequence the women looked to Morton to have something of an ambivalent manner about them in their dealings with him. They honestly could not make him out at all.

Despite their uncertainty, the women sensed that here was a man who would do them no harm and was, moreover, an honoured guest. While he stood among the women, letting them look at Robert, stroke his cheek and smile at him, a man came up to them. Although he looked to be pure Indian, his English was as good as Morton's own.

'I am to tell you what is said tonight,' this man said. 'To translate, you understand. You wish to say something, you tell me and I will say it for you.'

'That's right good of you. What should I do now? I'm not sure that this little one . . . ' Morton indicated the baby, 'will appreciate staying awake late.'

'This is not a problem.' The translator or interpreter spoke rapidly to one of the women and then turned back to Morton. 'This woman says that she would be pleased to care for your child tonight. You can trust her, she has had many children of her own.'

Morton felt embarrassed because he was afraid that these people would take his hesitation as a sign that he didn't trust an Indian to look after the baby well. It was nothing of the kind. Having been tricked once out of the infant, by Lone Wolf's mother, he did not especially wish to repeat the experience. These people, though, struck him as trustworthy and honest, so he handed Robert over to the woman, saying: 'Be sure to take good care of him, if you please ma'am.'

After he had handed the child over, his guide led him to the fires that had been kindled for the feast. As they strolled side by side, the Indian said: 'Not every white man would have called one of our women, ''ma'am''

For a moment, Morton was puzzled.

'It's just what you call a lady when you're talking to her,' he said. Then he understood what the man was driving at and added, 'Oh, you mean on account of she's Indian? Makes no odds to me, the colour of a man or woman's skin. It's what they are inside that matters.'

A long, narrow pit had been dug in the dusty soil and a fire kindled in it. As far as Morton could make out they would be sitting around the fire, as though it were a table. It made sense on a chilly evening such as this to have a big fire going; it was also more cheerful.

There was a new moon this night, which meant that apart from the light of the stars the sky was dark. A bright, cheerful fire would be just the thing.

'Is there anything I should know? Manners and such?' Morton asked his guide as they came near to the fire.

'It's polite not to refuse anything offered,' said the man. 'Other than that, no.'

'Tell me, where did you learn such good English?'

'I was raised by missionaries. I went to one of their schools.'

The man Morton knew as Stormcloud was standing by the fire, talking quietly to a few other warriors. When he caught sight of Morton, he broke off his conversation and came over at once.

'Morton,' he said. 'Morton.'

Jack Morton bowed, as though he had been introduced to an officer or something.

'It's good to see you again, Stormcloud,' he said.

The Indian spoke at some length, looking into Morton's eyes as he did so. When he had finished, the man who was acting as translator spoke.

'Stormcloud says that since you rescued his daughter, she is yours as much as his,' he told Morton. 'He says that you are responsible for her as well.

That is the Comanche way. If you save somebody's life, then it is like ... I think the word is 'adopting' that person. You understand?'

'I understand well enough. Is there any way that I can tell Stormcloud that I don't see the matter from the same angle, without causing terrible offence?'

'No.'

The meal was pleasant enough and not the ordeal that Morton had feared. The men all sat at their ease on the ground and passed platters of baked meats around, with great quantities of cornpone. There was also some kind of beer, which Morton didn't really take to but thought that it might have been discourteous to decline. He was, in fact, becoming more relaxed and cheerful than he expected, until a lone figure approached the fire and spoke harshly, while staring fixedly at Morton. In a low voice, almost a whisper, the man who was interpreting what was said for Morton, said: 'This man is Kiowa. He says he is looking for a white man who did a very bad thing to his mother.'

'His name wouldn't be Lone Wolf, I suppose?' Morton replied, also in a whisper.

The interpreter shot him a penetrating glance.

'I see you are the one he is seeking,' he said.

Stormcloud got to his feet and began talking. He spoke slowly at first, becoming more eloquent as he continued. He was not angry, but used a quiet, reasonable tone. When he had finished, the man at Morton's side said: 'Stormcloud has told this Kiowa chief that there is no white man here. He says that his brother is here, the blood relative of his only daughter and that if anybody touches a member of his family, then Stormcloud will use his whole clan to defend that person.'

Lone Wolf spoke a few more words, then turned on his heel and walked back into the shadows, giving Morton a venomous look as he left. Morton asked what the Kiowa's parting words had been and was told that they were simply an expression of acceptance of the state of affairs.

'So you think that will be the end of it?' he asked.

'No,' said the Indian, 'not if I know Lone Wolf. He wants your scalp hanging from his belt.'

The feast carried on after Lone Wolf left and, as far as Morton was able to see, nobody had been at all put out by the interruption. He ventured to ask about this and received confirmation that, as he had suspected, it was not uncommon for some challenge or insult to be delivered at such events as this.

'Some say that it is not a true feast unless a man is slain during it,' explained the Indian. 'Nobody here is surprised to see a Kiowa trying to begin a blood feud.'

''Long as it's not cast a dampener on this meal.'

'They've forgotten it already. Lone Wolf is boastful. He has no friends here.'

Morton calculated that it must have been long after midnight when the party broke up. Before he left Storm-cloud embraced him and declared again publicly that he owed a great debt to Morton. Then his guide went with him to collect Robert.

The baby was sound asleep in one of the wickiups. Morton picked the child up gently and, after bidding farewell to the man who had sat at his side throughout the evening, he made his way back to the comanchero encampment. A little before he reached it, a figure emerged from the shadows and he saw in the faint light from the stars that it was none other than Lone Wolf, wanting, presumably, his blood.

The two men stood facing each other for a few seconds, before Morton spoke.

'I don't know if you understand English or not,' he said. 'You feel you've cause to demand satisfaction from me. There's something to be said on both sides there, but I'll warrant you're in no mood to debate the rights and wrongs of the thing now. You want my blood.'

The other man said nothing, just standing ready and easy.

'This poor child has no part in this,' Morton continued. 'Come now with me to my van and let me set him comfortable and then we'll fight if you wish. Though God knows, it's not my wish.'

Not knowing if the man would suddenly leap at him and cut his throat, Morton walked on towards where he had concealed his van.

He was aware of the Indian walking after him. Since there was no move to attack him at once Morton was hopeful that he would at least be able to tuck the child up before facing this man in deadly combat. That prospect was not an enticing one. He was a dab hand with firearms and swords, but close-quarter fighting was not really his speciality.

A fire was burning a little way from the van and around it sat Emile Robarts and four or five other men. Robarts called out to him: 'Hey, Morton! How'd your famous banquet turn out in the end? Not too formal for you?'

'It went well enough, thanks.'

'Who's your friend there?'

'Fellow called Lone Wolf. He feels he requires satisfaction of me. But he was decent enough to let me tuck this little fellow up safe for the night first.'

Robarts got to his feet and drew his pistol, cocking it as he did so.

'Robarts, no!' Morton said urgently. 'I wouldn't have this man feel as though I'd led him into a trap. He was good enough to give me leave to put the baby to bed before we set to. I won't have him interfered with since he's played fair. He wants to fight me, we'll fight. Let him be.'

'We'll make sure there's no treachery,' said Robarts grimly, 'if you're determined on this.'

'I'm not so determined myself, but this man seems to be.'

Lone Wolf stood perfectly still and at

his ease as Morton pulled some of the brushwood aside and clambered into the back of his van. He put the sleeping child down and wrapped him carefully in the blanket. Then he jumped lightly down.

'Well my friend, I'm ready when you are,' he said to the waiting Indian. 'What's it to be, hands or knives?'

Robarts and the others had left the fire and wandered up to see how this was going to be done. When Lone Wolf drew a knife from the sheath at his belt, Robarts stepped forward and offered Morton the Bowie knife that he always carried himself.

'You sure you don't want us to settle this another way?' he said quietly as he handed it to Morton.

'It's kind of you to offer, but no,' replied Morton. 'I reckon he deserves a chance to show me what he thinks.'

Then there was no time for any more talking, because the man who wished to take Morton's life stood waiting, his knife in his hand. With great reluctance

Jack Morton turned to face him. The comancheros retreated to give them room and the two men began circling each other warily, looking for an opening.

This was not the first knife fight that Morton had been in, but the others had been more casual, less deadly affairs, in which the aim really had been to shed a little blood in order that honour was satisfied. Once a wound had been made an affair had ended and the men concerned had shaken hands.

This was another thing entirely and Morton knew the difference. Lone Wolf's whole standing was at stake here, because if some stranger could march through the land, tie up his mother and gag her, then where was the chief's authority? Doubtless, he was genuinely annoyed with the white man for the affront offered to his mother's dignity, but there was far more riding on the outcome of this little struggle than that alone.

If a chief could not maintain order in

his territory and protect his women, what sort of leader was he, anyway? Unless Lone Wolf succeeded in killing him Morton guessed that that particular clan of Kiowa would probably be looking for a new leader before long.

Then Lone Wolf lunged at Morton with his knife and the life or death battle had begun.

9

The man he was fighting was as muscular, swift and lithe as a mountain lion. Morton was keenly aware that if their contest went on for too long he himself was likely to be the loser. He lacked the Indian's stamina and speed, for one thing, to say nothing of the fact that it had been several years since he had even held a knife for any purpose other than cutting up the food on his plate.

Lone Wolf, on the other hand, moved as though the cruel steel blade was an extension of his arm. With a sinking feeling of dread, Jack Morton knew that it would take a miracle to save him from the man who was so determined to shed his blood and take his life.

After the first lunge, which Morton had dodged adroitly enough, Lone Wolf contented himself with moving round his adversary with his knife held out before him. In books, it is always a simple enough matter to scoop up a handful of sand and throw it in the other fellow's face, so blinding him and giving you the opportunity to move in for the kill.

In real life though, bend down and start fooling around like that, and you are liable to find that the man you're fighting has leaped forward and cut your throat. The whole practical aim of knife fighting is never once to let your attention wander from the knife being wielded a few short feet away.

One key factor in a knife fight is to watch your opponent's eyes, so as to gauge what he might be about to do next. In the darkness, illuminated only by the flickering light from the fire, this was all but impossible: both men were compelled to guess what the other was about. As they circled round each other, looking for some slight advantage, Morton knew that the lazy and self-indulgent lifestyle that he had pursued for the last two or three years had not been the best preparation for deadly combat of this sort.

When the Indian sprang the move came as a complete surprise to Morton. He jumped back quickly, but his foot caught on a rock and he went sprawling on his back. As if that were not bad enough, the Bowie knife that Robarts had loaned him flew from his hand as went down heavily. Lone Wolf saw this and his exultation was plain, even in the near-darkness. He moved forward for the kill and as far as Jack Morton could tell, there wasn't a damned thing to stop him.

Yet it was at that precise moment that Lone Wolf, Kiowa chief and undefeated warrior of any number of single combats and pitched battles, died instantly. All that Morton knew was that there was a blinding flash and a mighty roar, as though a bolt of lightning had struck close at hand. Then he saw his erstwhile enemy flying through the air and being dashed on to the rocky face of the canyon. The first explosion was followed almost instantly by another, further away. Morton understood what was going on.

'General Sheridan's calling cards!' he muttered under his breath.

He got shakily to his feet. Any man who has resigned himself to dying in the very next second, cannot help but be shaken and awestruck by the experience. One moment he had been lying there, waiting for Lone Wolf to cut his throat; now the Indian had been smashed to pieces and he, Jack Morton, was standing here alive.

'Bastard's using canister,' he muttered to himself, 'Against a civilian encampment too, from the look of it. Well, what d'you expect of the Yankee army?'

Morton's eyes fell upon the shattered remnants of the comancheros who had been spectators to his late duel. The canister shot must, by a singular stroke of ill fortune, have landed right among them. Every man Jack of them was dead. Only his lying prone like that had saved his life. All seven of the men who had been standing near to him had been killed instantly.

Again, in the distance, Morton heard another roar, as Sheridan's artillery let fly another ranging shot. At a guess, once those boys had the correct range they would saturate this whole area with alternating round-shot and canister, which would be none too healthy either for him or for Robert. He needed to take that baby and get out of there as soon as could be.

When he went to the van, however, Morton discovered that a stray piece of metal from the shell had scythed through one of the wheels, rendering it unfit for use. Inside, Robert had been woken up by the crash of the explosion and was crying softly. Morton gave him a dried crust to chew on and then picked up the bag containing food and diapers. He didn't see that he would be able to carry much else. At the last minute, he popped his pistol into the bag as well, but decided to leave the rifle behind.

From a cunning hiding place built into the side of the vehicle he removed some gold coins, which amounted to his savings since his snake oil business had begun. Just over $600 might not be a fortune, but it would perhaps set him up in another town. It was a shame to abandon all the snake oil and, indeed the van itself, but there was little enough to be done about it.

Morton jumped down from the back of the van and made his way to where the comancheros kept their horses and tack. It seemed a scurvy trick to play on them but, when all was said and done, the owners were now dead and unlikely to be needing either saddles or horses again, at least not in this world.

The cannon fire was steady now and more accurately targeted. The aim was probably to exterminate the Comanche village and do away with every man, woman and child living there. It had taken the army some years to get round

180

to this corner of the country, but now that they had they would be expecting to do a thorough job.

He had nearly reached the little corral when a rider loomed up from the darkness. In the normal way of things, Morton would perhaps have heard the beat of hoofs as it approached but, with the constant cannonade, the noise had been masked. Morton's hand snaked into the bag he was carrying, fumbling for his gun.

Then he realized that he knew this man and that he was very far from being an enemy. It was Stormcloud. Not only Stormcloud; his little daughter was perched in front of her father, looking terrified out of her senses.

'I didn't hear you coming there,' Morton told the rider. 'You fleeing as well, hey?'

Stormcloud's English was about as rudimentary as could be, but it was sufficient for him to get across to Morton that fleeing was the last thing on his mind.

'I fight. You, child, go,' he said.

'Yes, that's right. I'm taking this child out of here.'

'No,' said Stormcloud sharply. 'Child.' Here he lifted his daughter from where she sat in front of him and said again, 'Child go.'

'You want me to take your child? Is that what you're saying?' There was another rumble of artillery, like the thunder of a storm when it is slowly drawing nearer. 'I can't do that. I can't take your child away.'

It was hard to know how much of this the Indian understood, but when he spoke again, there was a distinct note of pleading in his voice.

'Morton. Morton,' he said. 'I fight. You, child go now.'

Under his breath Jack Morton muttered something to the effect that this was an unlooked for hindrance, but he nevertheless went over to the rider and said: 'Yes, I'll take the child. Although Lord knows what will be the consequence of this folly!'

The words were no sooner out of his mouth than Stormcloud lifted up his daughter and handed her down to Morton.

'Fight now,' he said. Next moment, he had spurred on his horse and vanished into the night, leaving Jack Morton with a baby in his arms and a little girl who could be no more than four years of age standing sobbing by his side.

'I don't know if you understand me or not,' Morton told the girl, 'but we need to be moving pretty sharpish here. Take my hand now and we'll get one of those horses tacked up and ready to get out of here.' In a lower voice, he said, more to himself than to the child: 'And as for what will happen to us after that, your guess is as good as mine.'

When they got to the corral Morton gestured that the girl should sit on the ground. He set down his bag and then handed Robert to her, saying: 'Hold the baby for me, will you?'

While he was tacking up one of the

horses, which was no easy task in the dark with the crash of artillery nearby, Morton tried to fathom out the best course of action. In addition to the booming of the cannons, he could also hear the crackle of rifle fire, along with pistol shots. It sounded as though General Sheridan and his men weren't having it all their own way during the assault on the Palo Duro canyons. The difficulty lay now in leaving the field of battle. If he knew anything at all about such actions, the soldiers now would be fired up to bloodshed. They would most probably shoot out of hand anybody they came across. A rider heading towards their lines would not have much of a chance. Hadn't he seen a track or something of the kind winding up into the hills, when Robarts had brought him here? The question was, could he find it now, without good light and with a battle raging around him? There was only one way to find out.

'Can you sit on that horse, if I lead it along?' asked Morton of the little girl, who looked at him blankly. He squatted down beside her and laid his hand upon her head.

'Listen honey,' he said patiently, 'there's little time to lose. We need to be digging up and leaving this place right now. I'm going to set you on horseback and hope that you'll be able to hang on to the reins without falling off.' Morton smiled at the child and she ventured a timid little half-smile in return. He wondered if she remembered him and understood that it was he who had saved her life when she was drowning.

Gently, he lifted the baby from her arms and set him on the ground, well clear of the horse's hoofs. Then he lifted up the little girl and placed her on the saddle, putting her hands on the pommel.

'There now,' he said. 'Just you hang on to the saddle and happen we'll do well enough.'

As the little group made its way to where Morton thought that he could remember some sort of path or track, the noise grew in intensity. He could see shadowy figures running about some way from them and the whole scene was illuminated from time to time by flashes of vivid light from the explosions of canister shot. These threw the combatants into view, frozen for an instant, like figures in a tableau or diorama.

The little girl appeared to be used to the rocking motion of the horse as they made their way up the slope. Morton kept an eye upon her, but she seemed to know what she was about. Mercifully, Robert was asleep, which meant that Morton could concentrate on holding the reins and making sure that he would be able to take control of the beast if it became spooked by the gunfire and cannonade.

At length they gained the heights and found themselves on the edge of a plateau. Morton paused for a moment and looked back at the network of canyons that they had left behind. It was a vision of hell. Fires were raging in a dozen spots and the flashes of artillery fire continued. In between the booms of the cannon and the explosions that followed he could hear the cries of men and the screaming of women and children. Those Yankee bastards were clearly making quite sure that the Indians got the message. Morton had an idea that the shattered remnants of the clans might be quite willing to be herded into reservations after a day or two of this slaughter.

'Well, child,' he said to the girl, who was also gazing down at the carnage below, 'for good or ill, looks like you and me are stuck with each other for a spell. I'm not altogether certain how I came to end up like this. Still, it can't be helped. I guess we will all of us have to make the best of it.'

Although he was convinced that the Indian girl could not understand a word of what he was saying, Morton found that it helped him to formulate his plans when he spoke out loud in this way, so he continued: 'Here's what I propose, little one. We head north along this ridge, keeping out of sight of those below. I don't want those idiots to get it into their heads that we are scouts or some such, else they will be firing their damned cannons up at us. When we find a track descending, we will take that and do our best to reach Claremont in that way. I should be able to unload this infant there on his kin, but as for you, the case is not at all clear. I can't just abandon you, but I really can't take responsibility for you for the rest of my life, as your father seemed to think. It's a thorny question.'

Perhaps the girl had slept before the attack began, but she showed no signs of weariness as the night passed. By dawn Morton was dog-tired, but the child sat on the horse, looking curiously from side to side. Not long after the sun rose a slight indentation to the left gave Morton reason to hope that there might be a way down from the plateau: a track, which might join the road to Claremont.

He lifted the little girl down from the horse.

'You sit here and wait,' he said. He emphasized these words with gestures until she was seated. Then he handed her the baby and crept cautiously to the edge to see what was going on on the plain below. The answer was, to his great relief, nothing at all; the road lay like a ribbon, quite clear. He went back to his little group of dependents.

'Come on,' he said. 'The way is clear. We'll move down as quick as we can.'

With the girl mounted once more on the horse and with him clutching Robert in his arms, they made their way down the narrow trail and eventually reached the road. There, Morton paused for a moment.

'Well,' he said, 'I reckon we're on the right trail now. With a little good fortune we might have a clear journey now to Claremont.'

As he finished speaking Morton became aware of a very faint rumbling, far off to the south. He stared in that direction, then his heart sank when he realized that a column of cavalry was moving smartly towards them. They weren't out of the woods yet; not by a long sight.

'Listen,' he said to the Indian girl, 'you need not be afeared, but these fellows might not be well disposed to you. Or me neither, if it comes to that. Just you stand there, looking as helpless as you are able, get it?'

As the troops came onwards the rumbling and creaking grew more distinct and Morton knew that there were not just horses in this unit, but also heavily laden wagons. *Artillery, most likely*, he thought to himself. So it proved as the column came abreast of them. It struck Morton that the smartest move that he could make would be to try and make himself and his fellow travellers as significant as possible. There was no point in trying to hide; that would only invite attention. Rather, he moved to one side and gave the road to the troops, just walking along by the side of the road, leading the horse with the little girl sitting in the saddle.

It very nearly worked. A squadron of cavalry passed them by without incident, then a gun carriage and limber. Morton was congratulating himself on his cunning when a mounted officer called to the team of horses pulling a field gun behind him.

'Halt! Pass word back, we're halting.' There was shouting and swearing as the message was transmitted along the length of the column. Morton thought that it might be wise if he were just to continue plodding ahead, but the officer called to him: 'You there. Stand to. I want words with you.'

Morton turned round, contriving to assume an expression of bewilderment and surprise.

'Who, me?' he asked.

'Yes, you. Who else did you think I meant?'

'What can I do for you?'

'Where have you come from?'

'We're just making for Claremont.'

'I didn't ask where you were going. I want to know where you've been.'

Morton could see that the entire column of cavalry and artillery had now halted and that this was wholly on account of this damned officer's interest in him. It was a complication that he could well have done without. While he was framing what he thought might be a suitable response to the artillery captain's question, that individual spoke again, saying: 'Do you know what I think?'

'I couldn't begin to guess,' replied Morton.

'I think you're one of those comancheros whose nest we just burned out back in Palo Duro.'

'Me, a comanchero? Nothing of the sort. It was those boys who waylaid me on the road a while back. I got no reason to love them.'

'Then how come you're travelling with an Indian child?'

Racking his brains frantically for a

suitable answer, Morton finally said: 'After I was bushwhacked I took to those hills over yonder. I found this child wandering there and couldn't leave her to fend for herself. So I brought her down with me.'

That his life was in peril Morton knew very well. These men were on active service and he imagined that martial law had been declared across this part of Texas. If they truly believed him to be a comanchero, perhaps a spy for them, then the best he could hope for would be a drumhead court martial and probably a firing squad at the end of it. The captain was staring hard at him and Morton wondered if he was trying to decide what size he took in coffins.

'What about the baby? Where does that fit into the scheme of things?'

'It's by way of being a long story. I'm sure that a busy man like you has more important things to attend to than my doings.'

'You let me decide for myself what I

have time for. What's your name?'

'Morton.'

'Is that your given name or your surname?'

'Surname. My Christian name's James, though mostly I'm known as Jack.'

'And you give your oath that you aren't connected with the comancheros over in the canyons?'

'I'm no comanchero.'

'Well then, for the sake of the children who are with you, I'll lend a hand for to get you to Claremont. You and those two can ride in one of the supply wagons and you can eat with us. Your horse can walk along of the wagon.'

'That's right good of you, Captain. You're a real Christian.'

It was a great relief to be able to sprawl at his ease in the open wagon, and it struck Morton that the girl was also pleased not to have to hang on there, stuck up on a horse. Now that they were relaxing it occurred to him that he didn't even know the child's name.

He pointed at his own chest and said clearly, 'Morton.'

Then he pointed at her and made a dumb show of bewilderment. It took her a second to catch his drift, but when she did she joined enthusiastically in what she obviously regarded as some species of parlour game. The girl pointed at Morton.

'Morton,' she said. Then she touched her own chest and said something which sounded very much to Morton like 'Keyhole'.

He pointed at her and said, 'Keyhole?'

This time, she smiled brightly and said definitely, 'Keyhole.'

'Well,' said Morton, 'I dare say as I ain't pronouncing it precisely in the Comanche way, but if you'll answer to 'Keyhole', then 'Keyhole' it shall be.' He stretched out his hand and engulfed her tiny one in his.

'I'm very glad to know you, Keyhole,' he said.

The captain still had some kind of

reservations about Morton, for he rode back along the column once or twice to speak to him. The first time he did so, he remarked: 'You're more lacking in curiosity than any man I ever yet met in the whole course of my life, Mr Morton.'

'How's that?'

'You encounter a column of troops on active service, who have quite clearly been in battle lately and you don't ask me a single question about what we've been up to. Anybody would think that you already knew all about the action.'

This was very close to the bone and so Morton prevaricated skilfully.

'Why, I don't take much heed of military matters these days. Had my fill of such things during the war.'

'I'll warrant from your accent that you weren't in the Union Army.'

'Shall we make Claremont tonight?' asked Morton, not wishing to enlarge upon his activities on behalf of the Confederacy.

'No, we'll camp up at dusk. Should

get there tomorrow afternoon.'

'I can't tell you how grateful I am for your assistance. I don't know how I would have managed unless you boys had chanced to come by.'

The officer looked at him and replied sardonically, 'I've an idea that you would have got along pretty well if left to your own devices, Mr Morton. You have that air about you of a man well able to paddle his own canoe.'

'It's kind of you to say so.'

'It wasn't meant to be in the nature of a compliment.'

10

The temporary camp that the artillery train set up when the sun had set reminded Morton very much of those he recalled from the war. The only difference was that these men were not really in a state of war. They went through the motions of posting sentries and so on, but this was done more to comply with the requirements laid down in textbooks on military tactics, rather than because they seriously expected an attack.

The reason being, thought Morton, that these bastards had been waging war upon peaceful villages containing women and children, rather than fighting an honourable war against an opponent who was also armed with artillery.

The rations the troopers shared with him were adequate, but not luxurious.

The men showed little interest in Morton and his two young companions. They had been told to offer him hospitality and that was what they were doing. Like their captain, these men entertained their own suspicions about this Southerner and the circumstances that had led to his being on the road here. Did they too think that he was an escaping comanchero who had somehow acquired those two children and was using them to help him project a tender and caring image and so cause others to help him on his way?

It didn't especially bother Morton to be cold-shouldered by the men who had so recently been butchering peaceful villagers, so he moved a little out of the way with his two young charges and began talking to Keyhole. She had the advantage of not understanding a single word that he said, so he was able to unburden himself of his hopes and plans, confiding in her the way that people sometimes unravelled their thoughts by talking to a cat or dog.

'You know, Keyhole, it's taken these last few days to show me how weary I've grown of this travelling life. Last two or three years I don't think I've stayed in one spot longer than three nights. First the river-boats, then that ridiculous van. I've forgot what it is to be settled and secure in one place.

'But I reckon I'm going to give it a try now. I've got better than six hundred dollars to get me started and I never was afraid of hard work if that was what was needed.'

While Morton talked to her, the little Indian girl played with the baby, who gurgled and smiled at her.

'Does that child's diaper need changing?' asked Morton. 'I guess I should do that before we sleep. What a mercy that I was able to wash those diapers in the river, back near your village.'

The girl he called Keyhole looked up at him and smiled. She seemed to take pretty much everything in her stride, that one.

'I should be able to rid myself of young Robert there,' Morton continued, 'but you're another study altogether, child; you know that? The good Lord alone knows what I'm going to do with you.'

To Morton's great surprise the girl reached out her hand and touched his cheek lightly. Then she carried on amusing herself with the baby. So the three of them sat, talking and playing, until it was time to sleep.

★   ★   ★

When he awoke the next day Jack Morton had a sense of foreboding which, as far as he was able to tell, was not founded upon any rational thought. On the face of it, everything was going just fine, but Morton had the distinct sensation that things were about to take a wrong turn. Lying there as he came to, Morton tried to work out what had

201

caused him to feel so. Had it been a bad dream, something he had eaten the night before? Try as he might though, he could not think of anything to explain his anxiety.

When the Indian girl woke up and stretched, Morton watched her unobtrusively. Like a startled fawn, the child looked around uneasily, almost as though she was sniffing the air for something. She too had caught the scent of danger.

'You feel it too, don't you?' Morton said. 'I didn't think I was imagining it. You keep close by me, you hear what I say? I'll take care of you, but you mustn't go wandering off or anything.'

Even if she couldn't understand his words, the child picked up Morton's mood and moved a little closer to him. He put his arm around the girl and hugged her.

'Don't you fret none,' he told her. 'We'll make it through all right, you, me and little Robert here. You let me know if you see or hear anything, yes?'

The artillery captain came by to see how they were before the column broke camp. Morton was intrigued to see that this man also was a little more alert than he'd been before. Was he too expecting trouble?

'God willing,' the officer said, 'we should be in Claremont a little after midday. I don't aim for to write you into my reports, Mr Morton. Do you now give me your solemn assurance that you mean us no harm and that you aren't a spy or something of that sort?'

'I'm no spy. I just want to get these children to safety, nothing more. Without wishing to appear ungrateful, I'll say this though, I don't think much of soldiers who make war on civilians.'

'I was only obeying orders,' said the captain, reddening slightly. 'I don't see as you have cause to complain. If not for us, I don't think you'd be doing so well now.'

'Like I say, I wouldn't wish you to think us ungrateful.'

The column moved off after a light

breakfast which consisted of nothing more than dry bread and watery coffee tasting of the tins in which it had been prepared. It was better than nothing, but Morton was beginning to look forward to a proper meal; preferably one served in a decent restaurant and accompanied by a drop of liquor. He'd had just about enough of roughing it.

Keyhole had also picked up the sense of something in the air. It had quite a different effect upon her, though, from what it had on Morton. For him, it was feeling of dread anticipation; for the little girl it was something exciting. Her eyes were bright and she chattered incomprehensibly to Morton, as though they were going on a Sunday School outing or something of that nature. He was glad enough to see her cheerful, but began to find her excitement a little wearing after a time.

'You know something we don't?' Morton asked the girl. 'I wish you could speak English, Keyhole. I've an idea that you might tell a rare story.

Anyways, let's get up on the wagon now. With luck we should all be sleeping in proper beds this night.'

Young Robert was inclined to be a little grizzly, so Morton applied a liberal amount of snake oil to the little boy's gums. The bottle was all but empty and Morton said: 'I hope we can find something in Claremont that works as well as this on your teething pains.' He laughed, shook his head and then said, 'All that time I'm peddling this stuff and pretending it'll cure anything from the ague to smallpox and there I was, sitting on the best patent remedy for infant teething pains that the world has ever known! If only I'd o' known.'

Morton was still finding it something of a novelty to be riding with a unit of the Federal Army. Not so long ago, these had been his deadly enemies and a band of artillery like this would have been a prime target for him and his men. It was slow moving, unwieldy and almost impossible to manoeuvre in battle. Yes, these field guns and their crews would have been like shorn lambs before him and his comrades during the war.

While these thoughts were going through his head, Morton noticed that little Keyhole's attention had been caught by something. She was staring intently to the right of the wagon.

'What is it, child?' asked Morton. 'Seen some animal?' He peered in the same direction that she was looking in, but could see nothing.

That the captain in charge of the column was feeling a little more nervous than he had been yesterday was shown by the fact that he had put out flankers when they set out: men riding a half-mile along either side, whose job was to keep an eye out for any ambush. After two hours of peaceful travelling it was beginning to look as though this had all been a needless precaution.

The land through which they were travelling was fairly flat and uninteresting. To the right were the red sandstone cliffs, behind which lay the canyons that made up the Palo Duro complex. Ahead were some low hills, topped here and there with wind-carved pillars of rock. The road was sloping down now, heading into a narrow defile that led between two rocky masses.

Morton's mind was beginning to turn now towards what would be the practicalities of his situation when once they reached town.

'First thing we'll need to do when we reach Claremont is make some provision for you,' he said to Keyhole. 'I can't be sharing living quarters with a girl-child; that would hardly be fitting. Although I can't say what we're going to do. I'm sorry for you, being orphaned and all, but I'd be less than honest if I didn't remark that you're a complication I could well have done without. Meaning no offence, mind.'

The little girl smiled at Morton, a bright, good-natured and open grin. She was obviously feeling pleased with life, which was, when you considered matters, very odd indeed.

While Morton was puzzling over this he noticed that one of the flankers who had been sent out by the captain was no longer mounted on his horse, but had fallen from the saddle and was being dragged along by one ankle. Even then, Morton did not catch on at once, but wondered why the fool didn't make any effort to free himself from the stirrup and remount his horse.

A fraction of a second later, the answer came to him: that the rider was dead and had been killed not by a gun, which even at that distance they would have heard, but probably by an arrow. In the time that it took Morton to put all this together, which was no more than a second or two, the attack began.

The Comanches along with their Kiowa allies had gathered a formidable force of horsemen together and ridden ahead of the artillery column, waiting patiently at the ideal point for an ambush. The riders had been concealed from view behind the rocky bluffs, which obscured the view of the road ahead. They had presumably been signalling to scouts on the cliffs overlooking the road, keeping themselves informed in this way of the progress of the army as it plodded north.

In retrospect, of course, it was absurd to think that the Comanches would allow anybody to massacre their families and burn their villages without seeking vengeance. Morton cursed himself for a fool, because he should have realized this and not allowed himself to accept help from the Yankees. How ironic if now he were to end up being killed alongside a bunch of soldiers of the Union!

As the riders streamed out from behind the rocky hills ahead of them the captain tried to arrange his men for defence. To his credit, he gave thought, even at this critical time, to the children in Morton's care. The officer rode up and said to Morton: 'I'm putting the wagons and guns in a circle. You and those children can stay there. You might be safe.' Before Morton could thank him, the captain had spurred on his horse and was off again.

Jack Morton had seen enough military engagements to know that this particular episode was not likely to end well for the soldiers. While the men were doing their best to move their various wagons, limbers and fieldpieces into a rough circle, the cavalry was milling about, waiting for orders that were not forthcoming. None of the troopers wished to take it upon himself to ride out and attack the Indians without specific orders to do so.

The horses that had been pulling the artillery were now unharnessed and the various loads were being pushed into position by sweating men. To Morton, this was quite mad. They would have done better to cut and run, leaving the heavy equipment behind. Then again, he supposed that the senior officer, at a safe distance from the battle, might object to field guns being abandoned and even allowed to fall into the hands of the Indians.

As he huddled behind a limber, his arms protectively around the two children for whom he was responsible, Morton reflected that all battles seemed to end up like this, with men shouting and running round like headless chickens. However the generals or the chiefs planned things, it always came down to frightened men shooting randomly at those on the other side. Sometimes the winner was the side whose men were less apt to run than their opponents, at other times it was because by good fortune one side happened to have more powder and shot than those they were facing. Seldom, though, were such engagements decided by military strategy or because of individual bravery. War was always confusion, chaos and mess.

In the present situation, the Indians were fighting to defend their territory, which always gave an advantage in battle. They had also had time beforehand to figure out what they would do.

The Federal forces, on the other hand, had had no thought of fighting until two minutes ago. *Unless I'm greatly mistaken*, thought Morton, *this will be a regular massacre.*

So it proved, as the riders harried the men who were on foot and trying to heave the wagons and guns into some kind of defensive arrangement. The cavalry, who should by now have been riding out and keeping the enemy at bay, were sitting and waiting for orders that did not come. They were firing their carbines at the attackers, which was good, but otherwise they were doing nothing.

It was impossible to say how many men were attacking the column. Certainly at least a couple of hundred, thought Morton. They weren't using lances and bows, either; all the riders appeared to be carrying rifles. The tactics the Comanches were using were pretty sound as well. They were moving swiftly, stopping every so often to fire at the men who were working to build the defences. While some were doing this, a group had split off and were beginning to draw near to the cavalry, trying to lure them into close-quarter combat.

At last the captain got round to issuing orders to the men on horseback. A bugle sounded and they formed up, ready to advance. Then, to Morton's amazement and horror, he saw that the men had drawn their sabres and were preparing to charge like that, with swords in their hands. He could only think that this was the standard army response to dealing with an Indian attack: to give them a taste of cold steel.

This would be all well and good if their foe was a rabble of savages armed with nothing more deadly than sticks and knives. That was not at all the case here, though, and sending swordsmen against men with rifles was, to Morton's mind, madness.

Although his main concern was to keep the children safe by hunkering down in the most sheltered spot, Morton occasionally risked a quick look around; every such glance confirmed his suspicions: that the soldiers were coming off worst. Those fools who had trotted off waving their sabres had, just as he thought they would, been cut down by rifle fire before they had much of a chance of using their brightly polished swords. The rest of the troops, including the captain who was, it appeared, the most senior officer present, were now in the crude ring of wagons, carts and ammunition limbers.

By chance, the officer commanding the column ended up right alongside Morton and his charges. He might have given the order for those troopers of his to ride out holding their sabres, but Morton could not help but notice that rather than draw his own sword, he was instead cradling a carbine. The shooting was now more or less continuous from both sides and Morton was wondering how much longer they had to live. He had, during the war, come across an army unit that had fallen into the hands of Indians and the memory of what had been done to those men haunted his thoughts for many days afterwards. The Indians were nothing if not inventive when it came to dealing with their enemies.

Still clasping the baby in his arms, Morton risked a look above the parapet. He gasped in astonishment. There, as large as life, was Stormcloud; wearing a magnificent war bonnet of eagle's feathers, which were dyed crimson at the tips. At the very moment that he recognized the Comanche warrior, the captain raised his rifle and prepared to fire. Instinctively, Morton knocked the rifle up, causing the shot to go wild. The officer turned to face Morton and in his eyes Morton could see the bitter confirmation of the suspicions that he had entertained about the man he had rescued on the road. The officer opened his mouth to speak, preparing to reproach Morton perhaps for his treachery, when a ball took him in the side of his head, sending him toppling sideways. Then

Stormcloud was shouting commands at the riders surrounding the makeshift stockade, and the firing raggedly died down, leaving an eerie silence.

Morton looked round and saw that not a single soldier remained alive. He supposed that he had been spared, because he had not been taking an active part in the fighting and nobody had thought to fire at him. Then a shadow fell upon him and he realized that a rider had come right up to the flimsy wooden barrier behind which he was cowering.

He looked up to see Stormcloud staring down at him impassively. The child he had come to know as Keyhole saw her father and, giving a squeal of delight, wriggled from Morton's arms and jumped up to greet her father. He smiled back at her gravely. Then he caught Morton's eye with his own and said quietly: 'Morton.'

'Well,' said Morton, 'I guess you'll be taking your daughter back again. She's pleasant company, but I won't deny I'll be glad to have only the one helpless infant to care for. I ain't cut out for to be a nursemaid and that's the fact of the matter.'

The other Indians watched this transaction impassively. There was no telling how much Stormcloud had told them about entrusting his daughter to the safekeeping of this white man. At any rate, it did not look to Morton as if he was about to be scalped this very minute, so he stood up, holding Robert carefully.

'Well,' he said to Stormcloud, 'if you could let me take one of the horses, I reckon I'll be on my way.'

At least one of the Comanches must have understood English, because a riderless horse was led forward: a cavalry mount. Just as Morton was about to step into the saddle little Keyhole ran up and flung her arms around his legs. He bent down and kissed the top of her head. Then, since there seemed no point in staying any longer, he mounted up, a little more awkwardly than usual for having the burden of an infant in his arms, and set off towards Claremont.

11

Even as he started north, leaving the massacre behind him, Jack Morton's mind was working furiously. He wasn't overly distressed at the death of those cavalry and artillerymen. After all, they had put themselves beyond the pale by their behaviour in Palo Duro. Even at the height of the War Between the States, when emotions were raging at fever pitch, neither side would have attacked villages like that, shelling women and children. No, as far as Morton was concerned those boys had got what was coming to them.

He might have his own private opinions on the destruction of that column, but Morton didn't expect everybody to feel the same way about it. There were those who would accuse him of not knowing where his loyalties lay if he were to express his honest views on the subject too openly.

This touched upon another question. It would be tactless and could even prove dangerous for him to ride into Claremont on a cavalry horse. There was an army brand on its rump and the saddle and ammunition pouches also declared that this animal and its tack were the rightful property of the United States cavalry. Once news of the massacre spread, it would be pretty unhealthy to be thought of as one who had had a hand in the business.

His musings were interrupted by Robert, who began whimpering.

'What's the matter, fella,' Morton asked him. 'Hunger, thirst, or pain in the teeth department?'

The baby was thirsty and probably wanted milk, but that had all run out now. All that Morton was able to offer was a few sips from the canteen attached to the saddle. In his bag was a few mouthfuls of the pap that the child lived on.

Morton looked up at the sun, trying

to gauge whether it was yet noon. He hoped that the officer who assured him that they would be in town a little after noon had been right. He truly didn't know what would happen if they were compelled to spend another night out in the open. He was himself tired of sleeping rough, but he feared that it might be the death of the child if he were not able to rest in clean sheets and be properly fed and watered soon. This was no sort of life for an infant.

After they had been travelling for perhaps an hour and a half Morton saw, shimmering on the horizon, what he at first thought might be a mirage; the kind of illusory visions that one sees on hot days in the desert. But it wasn't remarkably hot, nor was he in a desert. He reined in and scanned the distant landscape carefully. This was no mirage; the image was wavering only because of the warm air rising from the dusty soil that lay between him and his destination. This could only be the town of Claremont. It was not possible to calculate how far off he was from the town; it could be anything between ten and twenty miles. The high ground that the road passed through here gave Morton a view that extended a good long way ahead of him. Whatever the distance, it could hardly take him more than two hours before he was back in civilization.

For a moment, Morton was gripped with panic when he thought that he was unable to recollect the name of the man given to him by Robert's mother. That would be the hell of a thing, to fetch up in a strange town without any idea of what to do with the baby. He soon recalled the Christian name. Martin. It took some little time though to bring forth *Catchpole* from the deeper recesses of his memory. Martin Catchpole; that was one peculiar name, but it had the virtue of being distinctive. There probably weren't two men in that little town both of whom were called Martin Catchpole.

It was hard to know how he was to go

about this little errand. Without doubt, this Catchpole fellow would be pleased to see his grandson, but being simultaneously informed of his daughter's death might be calculated to take the edge off his pleasure in the family reunion. Perhaps, thought Morton, there would be some female relative who could be enlisted both to take charge of the baby and also break the sad news to the child's grandfather. That would be a perfect solution, all things considered. Jack Morton had never been one for a heap of wailing and weeping and he strongly suspected that there was going to be a mort of such things when he handed over the infant, along with the news of the circumstances surrounding his acquisition of the same.

When he was a mile or so from the outskirts of the town, having already passed a few farms, Morton dismounted and set Robert on the ground. Then he removed the saddle and bridle from the horse and sent the animal on its way with a slap on the flank. He would present an uncommon enough aspect as it was, entering the town carrying a baby, without the added complication of riding a horse that had been stolen from the US Cavalry. Morton was keenly aware that he cut a most disreputable figure, having lived and slept in these same clothes for some little while now. He had only the shoulder bag, which contained a couple of clean diapers for the child, a pot holding a little food and, of course, his pistol.

The odd looks and sidelong glances began as soon as he reached the streets of the town. Claremont wasn't a large place and most people living there knew, or at the very least recognized, one another. Not only was Morton a stranger, he looked like a disreputable vagabond. All this might have passed without remark, had it not been for the extraordinary fact that this tough-looking customer was cradling a baby. Such a sight had never before been seen in Claremont and it didn't take long for word to spread that there was a rare curiosity to be seen on Main Street.

Claremont was a respectable town, which managed in the general run of things to discourage hobos and drifters. Morton knew that his appearance contrasted sharply with that of the other folk he passed on the boardwalk, but there was little enough to be done about it. He could see women eyeing him askance and whispering to each other, while mothers called their children to them, presumably in case he should snatch them away and carry them off somewhere.

After a while he had had enough of this and was on the point of bearding the next passer-by and asking where Martin Catchpole was to be found. Before he could do so, a rival attraction appeared on Main Street, which drew attention away from Morton. Two black horses pulling a sombre, black-painted wagon approached, followed by a crowd of men and women dressed as though they were on their way to church. As the wagon drew closer Morton could see a pine casket lying in it, surrounded by flowers and wreaths of leaves.

Bowing his head in respect, Morton was relieved to find that people in the street had transferred their attention from him to the funeral as it passed. After the little procession had gone by he decided that the time had come to rid himself of his burden and to track down this young fellow's real kith and kin. He stopped an elderly party and asked where he might be able to find Martin Catchpole.

'Catchpole, did you say?' enquired the old man, 'Martin Catchpole? Why, you just missed him, son.'

'I did? Could you point him out for me, do you think?'

'Certainly. You see that wagon going along the way, with a heap of folk trailing after it?'

'The funeral? Sure I see it. Is Catchpole among the mourners?'

'No, my boy,' said the man, 'he has a

more important part to play than merely being one of the extras, as you might say. He has the starring role.'

'I don't rightly understand you sir.'

'Bless you, I thought I made my meaning clear enough. Martin Catchpole is dead. That there is his funeral.'

Jack Morton stared blankly at the old man, scarcely able to believe his senses. This was indeed an unlooked for development.

'When did he die?' he asked.

'Not above forty-eight hours since. Had the apoplexy and just dropped dead where he was standing.'

'Did he leave any kin?'

'His daughter was the only kin he had. She upped and left about two year since. Married some young fellow as Catchpole didn't take to. Rumour was that he cut her off without a cent. But what's your interest in the late and sadly lamented, if I might ask?'

'I have something of his. Doesn't he have any other relatives in town?'

'No; after his wife died some years

back there was just him and his daughter. They didn't get on right well, from all I heard.'

'Thank you for your help.'

Morton walked away from the old man almost in a daze. His plans had all centred around passing this infant on to somebody else and then going on his way. Now, that no longer appeared to be possible. He sat down on a log lying on its side that some thoughtful person had provided for those who wished to take the weight off their feet for a while. Robert was disposed to whine a little, so Morton took out the bottle of snake oil and applied a little to the child's gums. That was the end of the bottle. There was a very small amount of food remaining and he absent-mindedly spooned that into the child's mouth.

There were worse things that could befall a man than to be landed with a baby. When the Indians had attacked that column of artillery Morton had been quite convinced that he was going to die and yet here he was, still in the land of the living. He recalled how he'd tried to give up the child to the orphanage in Oneida and had found himself unable to do it. Maybe his conscience was stronger than he had bargained for. He knew as he sat there that he could not just abandon Robert and that, if it came down to it, he might have to care for the boy by his own self.

He addressed the child directly, trying to work out what he would do.

'It's like this, son,' said Morton. 'You and me are in a bit of a fix. This grandfather of yours looks to have died and I'm not sure how to tackle things now. Maybe he had friends that might help, do you think?'

As soon as he had said this it immediately seemed to Morton that he knew what to do. Raising a baby by himself might prove just a little beyond his powers, especially if he had to earn a living at the same time. He might, however, be able to manage it if he could rely upon a little help.

'Robert, my boy,' he told the child,

'I'm a fool. But talking to you has set me on the right path again. We need to go to a church.'

Nobody could have been more keenly aware than Jack Morton that his appearance was perfectly scandalous and that he was in no fit state to attend divine worship. This was, however, an emergency and he hoped that nobody would find it disrespectful for him to enter the house of the Lord in his present ragged and bloodstained condition.

Morton walked briskly along Main Street in the direction that Martin Catchpole's funeral cortege had taken. He soon came to a neat little burying-ground attached to an imposing church. There was no sign of anybody clustering round a graveside, and Morton was hopeful that he'd arrived in time to catch the mourners before their attention was diverted elsewhere.

The service looked to Morton as though it was drawing to a close. If he was going to make his pitch he'd best do it now. He was used enough to standing up in front of crowds and getting folk to buy his wares. He figured that this would be much the same as selling snake oil; only a little more important than trying to extract thirty dollars from a bunch of folks. He just needed to present the case in the right way. The only thing lacking was a shill to get the others in the crowd moving in the correct direction, but that couldn't be helped.

The minister had finished speaking and Morton took the opportunity to walk forward along the aisle towards the altar. There was dead silence as he reached the area beneath the pulpit and spoke to the minister.

'Hope you don't mind, Reverend,' he said. 'I just have a few words to say concerning this child.' The man looked too taken aback to utter any objection so Morton took his silence for consent.

'Folks, I take it that you all are friends or acquaintances of Martin

Catchpole, who I understand has lately died. This baby is his grandson.' There was a hubbub of shocked exclamations at that, which Morton allowed to subside before continuing with his pitch.

'I'm not seeking charity. I promised this child's mother to take care of him until I could get him to his grandfather. Since he's dead, my reading of the situation is that I am responsible for the boy from now on. What I would say is this. If any of you good people would like to help out here, then I'd be grateful.'

Nobody spoke for fully thirty seconds and Morton was beginning to think that he'd failed to make a sale. He was on the point of abandoning the enterprise and leaving the church when a woman in the front pew spoke up.

'That's really Sarah Catchpole's baby? I reckon I can look after him from time to time, if it's needful,' she said.

There was a pause, then a man said:

'My daughter likes babies, she'd be glad to help out.' Then it was like an auction, with everybody bidding at once and nobody wishing to be thought unwilling to do their bit for the orphaned baby.

'I got some baby clothes . . . '

'Got a cradle up in the attic . . . '

'You need a place to stay for a couple o' days?'

'I was at school with Sarah, I'll do what I can . . . '

The minister who had been conducting the funeral looked mightily taken aback by all this, but proved unwilling to be left out of the general outpouring of goodwill that had gripped his congregation.

'My wife will do what she can to help,' he said. 'I'm sure we all know what the prophet Amos had to say, as touching upon the widow and orphan and our duties and obligations towards them.'

After the fuss had died down the funeral continued and Jack Morton followed the mourners out to the grave for the interment. He had no clear plan for the future, other than to stay in Claremont for now. He had enough money to set himself up; he hadn't precisely decided as what. But with all the help he had been offered, Morton thought that things were likely to work out well enough.

He'd done with roaming for a while, that much was certain. It was true that a month ago, the last thing he'd been fixing to do was settle down and raise a child but, now it came to the point, there were worse things he could be aiming at. He said to the baby: 'Things will work out all right, little one. You see if they don't.'